Ashford

Melanie Rose

Copyright © 2011 by Melanie Rose

www.roseandwren.blogspot.com

All rights reserved. No part of this publication may be reproduced or transmitted in any form or by any means, electronic or mechanical, including photocopy, recording, or any information storage and retrieval system now known or to be invented, without permission in writing from the author, except by a reviewer who wishes to quote brief passages in connection with a review written for inclusion in a magazine, newspaper, blog, or broadcast.

The characters in this book are fictional and any resemblance to persons living or dead is purely coincidental.

Cover photo copyright © 2009 by Melanie Rose
Llandygwydd, Wales, UK

ISBN: 978-1466371736

Printed in the USA

For Mr. James Flower
In recognition of his unceasing encouragement and
excellent editorial assistance.
With my love.

ACKNOWLEDGMENTS

The BBC, for their wonderful online collection of firsthand accounts from the war

My aunt, Dr. Janis Caldwell, for being the first to find Perry as fascinating as I did

My husband, Aaron Huff, for his constant support of my obsession

1

My grandmother always said there were only two types of people, those who had class and those who did not. According to her rule, the man sitting opposite me in the train was obviously a person of the latter type, for he sprawled across his share of the seat in a way which would have horrified my grandmother, and his hair and clothes had a rumpled, unkempt look, as if he had dressed himself that morning in a great hurry without the aid of a mirror.

However, whatever my grandmother's opinion might have been, I found myself liking the man seated across from me. He was reading an Italian paper, and his long, straight nose was only inches away from the newsprint as he studied it. His light brown hair stood mostly on end, and it was not difficult to see why, for whenever he came to something in the paper that seemed to puzzle him he ran his fingers into his hair and pulled upwards, at the same time twisting his face into an expression of distress.

My Italian was not very good, limited to the short phrases which travellers learn in the last weeks before their departure, and the page of the paper facing me revealed nothing intelligible except one advertisement in the bottom right-hand corner which bore an illustration of a waiter with a steaming tray and the words "Pasta! Pasta! Pasta!" in bold capitals underneath. I considered that perhaps some great tragedy had occurred, for the strange man seemed to tug at his hair more often as time went on. I supposed that I shouldn't be studying him so carefully. It was rude, no doubt, to examine people on trains.

I glanced to my left. My chaperones, the Beauforts, were asleep. Mr. Beaufort's mouth had fallen open and Mrs. Beaufort was snoring in an allergic sort of way, which reminded me of the snuffling sounds my grandmother's pug, Sigurd, made. My grandmother had calmly stated when she said good-bye to me that the Beauforts had no class, but that they were kind and would at least take good care of me, for the sake of my dead parents if for no other reason. In their case I was inclined to agree with her. The Beauforts *were* kind, well-meaning, and completely tactless. They loved to stand in line for hours to see little stone monuments with names and dates engraved on them, and then to write them down in little notebooks with gold pens with "I have visited the Colosseum" engraved on them. They thought me uninterested, because when we visited the Pantheon or the Colosseum I had not questioned the guide about the cost of upkeep or the exact height of the arches, but had been silent. They could not know that I was standing in speechless awe, simply breathing in the air of those ancient places, feeling the pride of the builder in his creation, hearing the heavy breathing of the workers as they moved each stone into place, seeing it all as it must have been in its glory.

There was no one else in our part of the train. Outside it was completely dark, but I could not sleep like my companions. I waited, watching the window eagerly, for the dawn to come and show me what new landscape we were passing through.

Our travels had begun in Rome, and we had spent two weeks there before taking the train north to

Florence, where we expected to arrive by midmorning. After that we were to go on to Venice, and from there we would go west across the border into France and stop in Nice for a week or so. From there I was not sure of our course. I only knew that the Beauforts intended to continue going north as the summer went on, eventually crossing the English channel by boat and coming to Britain, where we would spend some time before catching another boat to transport us back to America and my Grandmother's tall, lonely house on the coast of Maine.

I was jerked out of my thoughts by a rustle of papers and the feel of something falling onto my foot. The man opposite, it seemed, had not been so wide awake as he had appeared, and had fallen asleep for a moment over his paper. It had fallen from his hands, along with a little book, which had bounced onto my weathered brown walking shoe. I picked it up, glancing at the title as I did so, and handed it back to him. He was awake again, gazing at the papers strewn over the seat and floor, and wondering, no doubt, how they had got there.

"Grazi, Signorina," he said, taking the book and stuffing it into his jacket pocket as if he were ashamed of it.

"Don't mention it," I answered in English, for his thanks, said as no Italian ever said it, as well as the title of the book, made me both bold and curious.

We had both whispered so as not to wake the Beauforts, and now he leaned closer, pulling the book out of his pocket again and looking relieved, and said in English, "I was afraid that silly thing would give me away. I've been trying to puzzle out this paper, but I'm afraid I've not had much luck with it." He glanced ruefully from the paper to the book, a small copy of an English-Italian dictionary.

I was usually timid with strangers, but the situation was unique, and it surprised me into sympathy.

"I know what you mean," I said. "I hardly know any Italian, and I don't like appearing ignorant. I wish I were more fluent. I love the sounds, just hearing it spoken in the street, but I can't make out one word in ten."

His only answer was to sit up straighter and clear away some of the paper which littered the seat beside him. He then inclined his head towards the empty space in an inviting sort of way, smiling cheerfully as he spread the paper out again on his lap.

I glanced a little uncertainly at the Beauforts, not quite sure what they would think, then shrugged my shoulders and took the seat which had been offered to me. After all, I thought as I considered the man beside me, we were in a public train, and he was a good deal older than I -- maybe thirty or so to my seventeen. Also, the Beauforts themselves were constantly pressing me to take part in what they called "socialising with the locals", a game which I had no taste for, having noticed that in the Beaufort vocabulary "socialising" was only a code word for "interrogating" while "locals" appeared to be a euphemism for "savage natives". This was different. The Beauforts were asleep, and I could not be embarrassed into silence by their remarks.

The last hours of darkness passed by swiftly as together my new friend and I, with the aid of his dictionary, tried to decipher the stories in the paper. The front page was dedicated to something to do with the German Nazi party -- a group of people about whom I knew very little then. To me Adolf Hitler was nothing but a small man with a loud voice and an unfortunate taste in facial hair. My grandmother pursed her wrinkled lips and frowned when his name was mentioned, but she had not been worried enough to put off our trip or change our travelling plans. Before the year's end that small man and his tasteless moustache would turn the world upside down, but for now he and his followers were just interesting enough to fill up a page in an Italian newspaper.

Even fascinating foreign papers grow a little tiresome eventually, especially when nearly every word must be carefully searched for in a pocket dictionary. After a while I could understand very well why my new friend had fallen asleep in the midst of his labour. Soon enough our talk turned away from the contents of the newspaper and moved to more general topics. I had never been very good at the conventional forms of small-talk, but the situation itself was hardly conventional, and with the Beauforts' curious eyes conveniently hidden under their lids, I talked freely to the stranger, asking and answering questions with an interest I had never felt so free to indulge before.

His name, he said, was Perry Bertram, and he was from a place called Nettlebridge in the west of England, somewhere between Bath and Wells. He had travelled to Rome for a few weeks of "idle enjoyment", which seemed to include walking eight miles or so a day and eating a great deal to balance out the exercise, and was now on his way home. When I told him that we had plans to stay in England for several weeks at the end of our journey he was very interested, and asked all sorts of questions about the places we intended to visit and how long we planned to stay. I could not answer most of his questions, for in those matters I was at the mercy of the Beauforts, but I told him that to the best of my knowledge we intended to travel extensively.

"Good," he said. "I'm glad to hear it. So many people make the mistake of thinking London is far enough. London is a wonderful city, of course, but it isn't all there is, by any means. Now, down in our part of the country--"

"Anna?"

It was Mrs. Beaufort's voice. I looked up, feeling the little panicky jump in my stomach which I felt nearly every time I heard her say my name, and the cowardice which was always the worst part of my nature asserted itself. I was silent, looking down at the pattern of my skirt, little grey curlicues against a green background, as if it were the most important thing in the world.

Perry Bertram saved me.

"Your charge and I were just passing the time," he said smoothly. "Long train rides can get so tedious. I'm sure you would agree."

Yes, I liked him, whatever Grandmother would say. He reminded me of my favourite uncle, my Uncle Nicholas. Already Mrs. Beaufort was won over, and was plying him with questions. Then Mr. Beaufort woke up and joined the conversation, pointing out how very important it was to discover, "where the locals ate" and eat there yourself, and from his tone and manner there rose in my head a picture of Mr. Beaufort on an African Safari, following a herd of elephants to their watering hole armed with a notebook and a little gold pen.

All the time I continued to shrink further back into my corner, feeling that my proximity to the Beauforts tainted me with a touch of their vulgarity, yet hating myself for the feeling. The sun rose beyond the window, bathing the beautiful Italian landscape in golden light, and I turned my eyes to watch it in relief as we passed through groves of twisted olive trees. Everything was fresh and lovely, green and gold and shining in the sun, and it made me long to escape from the confines of the train and run unhindered through the fields and over the distant hills. Who cared for a city, even Florence, when there were places like this?

But it was Florence, and not a far green hill, for which we were heading, and when we reached it I was not sorry, for it was beautiful too, though in quite a different way from the trees and fields we had left behind.

The train pulled in at the station and the passengers began crowding out onto the platform. We gathered our things and joined the mob. As we passed out of the station I heard a familiar rustling noise, and, looking around, saw my friend from the train, bending again to collect his scattered papers. He glanced up, caught my eye, and smiled, but Mrs. Beaufort was pulling me somewhere and I could only follow. Thus, so I thought, ended my brief acquaintance with Perry Bertram.

Melanie Rose

Ashford

2

It was wonderful to wake up in my own room of our Florence hotel, refreshed from a good night's sleep and eager for the day ahead. I climbed out of bed and went to the window, flinging open the shutters and leaning out at a dangerous angle, careless of the five-story drop below, and felt the cool morning breeze brush against my face. It was still early, and the window only looked out onto a narrow back street, but a few people passed beneath even at that hour, and one, a tall woman in blue, looked up at the window. For a moment our eyes met, and she smiled. I smiled back, overwhelmed by that feeling of kinship with the whole world which comes the first time you connect with something or someone beyond yourself or your immediate circle. Language, birth, nationality -- what were they but flimsy barriers people put up to hide themselves from the rest of the world? People were just people, after all, no matter where you found them. We were all the same, just trying to sort out the everyday conundrums which twisted our lives into question marks. The least we could do was acknowledge it.

With these thoughts I shut the window again and dressed myself, full of joyous expectations for the days ahead. I even hummed to myself as I brushed my hair, half dancing my way between the bed and the dresser. It was a glorious day. The sun was shining. I was in Florence. What more could anyone wish for?

Mrs. Beaufort's knock at the door brought me back to earth, or at least a little closer to it, and I realised that there were still one or two small things I could find to wish for. But even the presence of the Beauforts could not do much to dampen my spirits, and I remained in a cheerful temper, though somewhat subdued, as I followed them downstairs to breakfast.

The dining room of our hotel was a comfortable place, beautiful in the same way all places which provide nourishment are beautiful, no matter how different their outward appearance. The tables were covered in brilliant white tablecloths, and fresh flowers were everywhere. There were many small tables for groups of two or four, set around the outside edges of the large room, for those choosing to keep to themselves; and two long tables in the centre for those bold individuals who chose to brave the society of their fellow tourists.

The Beauforts, as bold individuals, seated themselves at one of the long tables, and I followed, feeling a little bolder than usual myself. I was still not keen on playing "socialise with the locals" but I was certainly prepared to watch and listen.

My eyes wandered over the room, searching for interesting faces. There was a group of elderly men at one end of our table, arguing in Italian and gesticulating wildly (and rather dangerously) with hands still gripping knives and forks. At the other end was a group of French women. The higher notes of their chattering voices, mixed with the deeper tones of the men, turned the usually musical sounds of the two languages into one inharmonious cacophony, over which it was impossible to hear anything else. Most of the remaining company did not even attempt to compete with the noise, and ate in silence, but a few, including the Beauforts, started up a telegraph of yells and hand gestures across the room, passing volleys of information on what to see, how much to tip the drivers, and where or where not to eat. One, a grey-haired man of about seventy who spoke only a little English, kept yelling from the other side of the room, something about a tower, but since only one word in ten was intelligible nobody knew which tower he was referring to. Finally, as they had finished their breakfasts, his wife took him by the arm and led him away upstairs, while the Beauforts, exhausted by their energetic attempts to understand him, settled down to imbibe espresso and pastry in great quantities and discuss between themselves whether to visit Santa Croce or the monastery of San Marco after breakfast.

I too, having finished my survey of the room, turned my concentration to my food and thoughts of the day ahead. Through the dining room windows I caught glimpses of a glorious expanse of sky, from which beams of sunlight shone down on the roofs and spires of the city, turning it into a shining thing of blue and gold. Beyond I could see a sort of green haze, which spoke to me of the hills among which the train had brought us the day before. I could see no reason to wander the closed-in aisles of any building, even if it were the greatest of churches, when outside the sun shone so brightly and Something beckoned from those far away hills, pulling at me with such intensity that I longed to rise from the table that moment and answer its call. I actually reached down to grip the seat of my chair, as if my own weak hands could hold me down against the pull of that greater Something.

"Anna."

It was Mr. Beaufort. He had turned from his guidebook to look at me over his spectacles.

"Mrs. Beaufort and I are having some trouble deciding how to start off our time here in Florence. What do you think? Is there anything here that you particularly want to see?"

There it was. My moment had come. Mr. Beaufort had offered it to me -- my chance to choose what we should do. But the opportunity came so suddenly that I was not prepared for it. I paused and wet my lips with my tongue before I spoke. My hands were trembling. I grasped the chair harder. It was strangely difficult to put into words what it was that I longed to see.

"I don't know," I began, stumbling over my words, although I had known exactly what I wanted a few minutes before. "I would really like to, well, just sort of take in the city...I mean, it's a beautiful day...and maybe some of the countryside." My voice gained a little strength as I went on, but not enough. "Perhaps we could just wander, and enjoy the sunshine. It's a beautiful day."

Mr. and Mrs. Beaufort looked at me, nodding in a knowing sort of way which meant absolutely nothing. However, they had heard something, even if it was not exactly what I had intended to convey.

"It is an idea, my dear," said Mr. Beaufort, turning to his wife. "We should take full advantage of the sunshine. According to the guidebook there is a charming drive that takes you up around Fiesole. The guides are locals, you know. They take out groups of twenty or so at a time, but they don't leave until after lunch."

Mr. and Mrs. Beaufort then began to discuss how we should occupy ourselves for the morning.

"I believe the best thing would be to go to the Pitti Palace and the Boboli gardens," said Mrs. Beaufort, looking up from the guidebook. "We would have time if we set out at once, and the gardens will be out of doors, which should appeal to Anna."

Mr. Beaufort looked at his watch. "Ah!" he said. "We had better get going then. I suppose you'll need a few things from your room, Anna? Very well. We shall meet you in front of the hotel in exactly five minutes."

Ashford

I ought to have predicted this, I thought as I hurried to my room. In their kindness the Beauforts had sought to give me what they thought I wanted, and in their blindness they had not been able to see what that was. I was really to blame for this, for my words had been ridiculously inadequate. The result was that we were to rush off to the Pitti Palace and the Boboli gardens, collect information off plaques and view important monuments, stand where the signs told us to stand to see the best views, and be in such a hurry that we lost half the beauty of each place in rushing to the next one. Then we were to have a drive "up around Fiesole", a place I had longed to see, but not in the company of twenty other people with, again, a guide to show us where to stand and what to look at and tell us important dates from the history of Florence. Again, I was only getting half of what I wanted, but half would have to do. With the Beauforts I could never have my desire. It was not something they could understand, and I could not make them.

I wanted to be a part of the city, as I had felt that I was for that brief moment at my window before breakfast. I wanted to discover it for myself. I wanted to stand, looking out over Florence from Fiesole, and pick out its many beauties with my own eyes, seeing and admiring them, not for their age or size or the dates connected with them, but for themselves. But this was not to be while I was with the Beauforts, and they would never let me go out alone. Besides, it would have seemed ungrateful of me to suggest it when they had tried so hard to plan the day for my pleasure.

Quickly, I fetched my jacket from my room and tucked a little money away in its inside pocket. On the way downstairs I passed the door of the Beauforts' room. It was open, and the sound of their voices drifted out into the hall.

"Do you think we ought to bring our umbrellas dear? It just might rain later you know."

"We might as well, just in case. Don't forget the field glasses. And maybe we should bring our mackintoshes…"

The voices faded as I turned a corner and descended the curving staircase. I smiled in spite of my frustration. There was a window on the landing, and I paused to look out. The sun was still bright, the sky still blue, without a cloud to be seen. My smile broadened as I went out through the front entrance and settled myself on the top step to wait. The stone was warm from the sun. I closed my eyes and leaned against the railing to soak up the light and warmth. At that moment I would not have cared if the Beauforts had taken an hour.

Ashford

3

It was twenty minutes before I sensed that the Beauforts (laden with field glasses, umbrellas, mackintoshes, and other indispensable items) had materialised beside me. I opened my eyes, stood up, and we went down the steps to the street together.

The Pitti Palace was not far from our hotel, a fact for which I was grateful as it meant that we would walk there and remain in the open air instead of inside a stuffy cab. It was much more exciting to walk, and I absorbed colour, scent, and sound as we passed fruit and flower markets, street musicians on the corners, and narrow side streets which probably led only to narrower and dirtier streets but which in my imagination became enchanted avenues of mystery and adventure.

We crossed the Arno over the Ponte Vecchio. Between the shops lining the bridge I could catch glimpses of the river, glittering in the sunlight. The Beauforts had stopped to examine something in a shop window, and I walked to the nearest gap, away from the crowds, and looked out at the water, sending my silent thanks back to America, where my grandmother would be getting up and thinking about breakfast.

She had always taken care of me, ever since the death of my parents, bringing me up in her old-fashioned house, about which the combined smells of lavender and mothballs hung like musty remnants of bygone elegance. She had been a kind and loving guardian, though somewhat rigid, and in that moment, standing on the bridge, I began to realise just how much I owed to her.

The Beauforts, who had been turned aside by a distracting display of jewellery in a nearby shop, (or rather, Mrs. Beaufort had been turned aside and had taken Mr. Beaufort with her) returned to claim me and hurry me along with them. We would return another day. These quaint shops would be excellent places to shop for souvenirs, but we had no time now if we wanted to see half of what there was to be seen at the Palace and still have our afternoon drive.

At the Palace we disbanded, for Mr. and Mrs. Beaufort could not agree on what they wished to see first. Mrs. Beaufort longed to see the costume and jewellery displays. Mr. Beaufort preferred to take a survey of the outside of the building, to view the architecture and jot down estimates of the square footage in his notebook. I, having learned something from the morning, said nothing of what I wished to see, but at a certain crucial moment ventured the suggestion that we should separate for a time and each see what we chose before meeting again at an agreed-upon time and place.

"Are you sure, my dear?" asked Mrs. Beaufort, her brow puckering with worry. "We promised your grandmother we'd look after you. What if you got yourself lost?"

I swallowed the indignant reply which rose to my lips, then assured her that I would stay within the palace grounds and not wander too far. That settled, they seemed to find no further flaws in my plan. The time and place of our meeting were fixed, and we went our separate ways.

After wandering through the Palace and paying brief though awed tribute to its splendour, I took myself to the gardens. There I gave myself up to the loveliness of the day, and strolled through the park listening to the splashing of the fountains and admiring the trees, the brilliant flowers, and the view of the Tuscan hills glimpsed beyond through a warm purple haze. Near the Palace the gardens were rather crowded, but I wandered far through the park, seeking hidden corners and secluded paths, and there I spent the remainder of my time, with only the breeze and the sunlight and my own dreams for companions.

At the appointed time I returned to the spot designated for our rendezvous. I was there ahead of the Beauforts, but I was prepared to wait. Perhaps, I thought, Mr. Beaufort had found a guide to question about the square footage, or perhaps Mrs. Beaufort had been mistaken for a jewel thief and was now in the custody of the security staff. More likely they had just discovered the gift shop.

A smooth bit of green lawn stretched invitingly before me. I settled down to wait for my chaperones, lying on my back in the grass with my arms behind my head, and lost myself in imagination.

I was brought back to reality by a woman's voice speaking tentative Italian. I sat up as the speaker, a short, plump woman, in clothing more remarkable for colour than for taste, began to speak again.

"Signorina..." She seemed to be searching for the right words, and she waved her arms in a helpless sort of way. Her Italian was about as extensive as my own. I remembered Perry Bertram, and realised quite suddenly that by some strange mistake I had been chosen as an object in someone's version of "ask a local". I considered that in general tourists did not loll about on the grass daydreaming. We were not supposed to have time for it. The woman was still gesturing confusedly, and behind her a portly middle-aged man and a very pretty young woman with a great deal of brilliant red hair stood watching.

"Excuse me," I said, "but I am not Italian, and I don't understand much of the language."

Her arms relaxed again.

"Oh, I'm sorry. We were trying to find someone to tell us the way back to our hotel." The soft drawl of the woman's voice indicated that she must be from the southern United States, maybe the Carolinas or Georgia. "We've been in Florence for a week, and we thought we knew our way so we left our maps behind. It looks so tacky to be pulling them out all the time. But earlier this morning we came here, and now we can't seem to find our way anywhere else. We leave here and get turned around, and then the only thing to do is come back (because anyone on the street can direct you to the Palace, you know) and try to retrace our steps again."

The man and the young woman behind her nodded as she finished speaking as if to add credence to what she said. Searching the crowds beyond I saw the Beauforts approaching from the Palace and answered, "I can see my chaperones coming now. They always have maps with them."

The woman thanked me, and all four of us watched the Beauforts' progress across the lawn with interest. They had indeed discovered the gift shop. There was no mistaking it, for they appeared to be even more heavily laden than when we had parted, and I could not repress a little smile as I speculated on what the great discovery might have yielded this time.

The Beauforts did have maps, and were more than happy to help the strangers find their way back to their hotel. I waited at a slight distance while they puzzled over the maps, and was just losing myself in imagination again, staring at one window of the Palace and not really seeing it, when I realised that someone was standing beside me. Pulling myself out of my reverie, I recognised the young woman who had stood behind the colourful woman with the portly gentleman. She caught my eye and smiled.

Nobody could have withstood her smile. I certainly could not. Had I been a man I would have fallen hopelessly in love.

"What is your name?" I asked, suddenly feeling very childish.

"Gloria."

It suited her. At once we settled into conversation, and the actions and conversational topics of our elders were completely forgotten.

* * *

As it turned out, our collective fate did not lead us to Fiesole that afternoon. Instead, after a lengthy sojourn on the lawn by the Palace, it led us on a meandering walk through the streets of Florence in search of the Whildon's hotel (Whildon being the surname attached to the colourful lady and the portly gentleman). The Beaufort's map was detailed enough that it could have led us straight there, but with Mr. and Mrs. Whildon stopping to admire the view, Mr. and Mrs. Beaufort stopping to admire ornate paperweights in a shop window, and Gloria and I stopping to admire everything else, not to mention all of us getting lost in conversation with each other and missing the right streets, it took much longer and led us a strange winding way through the city.

By the time we did reach the Whildon's hotel it had already been arranged that we would meet the next morning and spend the day together. No idea could have been more welcome to me, and Gloria seemed pleased as well to have the company of another young person. The

Beauforts were always fond of socialising, and the Whildons were friendly, warm-hearted individuals and entered into the scheme with enthusiasm.

"Now that we've found your hotel," said Mr. Beaufort to Mr. Whildon, examining his watch, "don't you think it would be a good idea to find a nice little place to eat? I don't know about you and your wife and Miss Gloria, but *we* three missed our lunch."

Gloria and I smiled at each other as our elders began, all four at once, to discuss where to dine. Above the voices of the others I could hear Mr. Beaufort, saying to anyone who would listen, "I really think the best thing to do is ask a local. Just look around, and when you see someone who looks like a local pull them aside and ask them for directions to some quaint little place. Then we'll get something nice and authentic."

At first no one seemed to notice what he said, but after he had repeated it several times Mrs. Whildon looked at him and laughed. She had a cheerful, hearty laugh -- the kind that makes you want to laugh too even if you don't know what you're laughing at.

"Why, Mr. Beaufort," she said, "that would be a lovely idea, except that the last time I tried that method was just this morning when I accosted poor Anna for directions. If we could be sure of grabbing a local it would be another matter, but more likely we would just repeat the mistake and frighten another young tourist with a trick for blending into the landscape."

Everybody laughed, even Mr. Beaufort, and we set off down another street (not meandering this time, but walking quite quickly, for we were all hungry) in quest of some form of sustenance which would be agreeable to all.

It seems to be the peculiar fate of travellers to be unable to find anything at the time it is needed. That morning, as we had walked from our hotel to the Palace, it had seemed as though the whole city were filled with cafes. They had appeared on nearly every street corner, and we assumed that on our return we would simply find one we liked and dine there. Not so. Now, as we wandered the streets looking for somewhere to eat, the formerly numerous cafes frustrated our intentions by not appearing at all. We passed hotels, banks, churches, offices, and shops carrying everything from clothing to cookware to flowers, but nothing edible presented itself, although Gloria whispered to me as we passed a candle shop that she had heard you could eat beeswax and she was about ready to try it.

At last we stumbled upon a street market, and from among the stalls of flowers and cloth and jewellery drifted the aromas of bread and fruit. Led by the scent we sought out the food stalls from the others, and this time the Beauforts were not turned aside even once by notebook or pen, paperweight or jewellery. On this venture we all moved as one, and quickly loaded our arms with bread and cheese, some sliced meat and fresh fruit. Then we marched away in triumph with our spoil, munching a little on the way.

A low wall beside the Arno became our dining table. Gloria and I, perched on top of it, handed out food to our elders as they reclined on benches below. The river swirled beneath us, occasionally sending up a bit of spray -- just enough to brush our cheeks with the lightest of kisses. The sun warmed the stones of the wall on which we sat and touched Gloria's hair with a brilliance that was almost blinding. The afternoon was as close to perfection as any I had seen.

Melanie Rose

4

It did not take long for everyone to realise that we were better off as one group of six than as two groups of three. Suddenly the advantages of travelling together appeared as obvious as the advantages of wearing coats in cold weather. Everyone would enjoy the more varied company of a larger group and Gloria and I would each have the society of another young person. We were all travelling in approximately the same direction anyway, and when we wished to see different things we could split into convenient pairs. This last point was particularly attractive to Gloria and me.

"And it needn't be permanent, of course," Mrs. Whildon said kindly. "After all, we don't know each other very well yet. In spite of this favourable beginning we might realise after a week or so that we have nothing in common after all. If we do, we always have the option of splitting up and going our separate ways again."

The result of this discussion was an immediate removal from our hotel to the Whildon's, where we were lucky enough to find a vacancy. I was to share a room with Gloria, thus adding yet another advantage to the merging of groups: that of splitting the cost of three rooms among six instead of two among three.

* * *

"I don't know why they kept going on about the possibility of splitting up later," Gloria said to me that first night as we prepared for bed. "As if there could be any objection to the arrangement!"

It occurred to me that the Whildons might wish to have a way out of the deal if the society of the Beauforts disagreed with them, but I said nothing, only nodded agreement. Certainly, if the scheme concerned only Gloria and myself there would be no fault to find with it.

"It's part of being their age," I said, laughing. Then, standing with my arms folded I put on a didactic expression and quoted my grandmother. "'When you're making plans it's important to think of everything that could possibly go wrong before you come to a decision.'" I let my arms fall to my sides. "It's true I guess, but it's a wonder they ever decide anything at all."

That night did not see us in our beds until it was half over, and even then we stayed awake, whispering to each other and making plans for the morning.

I suppose it was the excitement of all this which deprived me of the greater part of my remaining allowance of sleep that night. I woke before the sunrise, completely purged of weariness in spite of the brevity of my rest, and scrambled out of bed. Gloria was still asleep, her long hair tangled on the pillow, beautiful even then. I tiptoed past her bed to get to the tall window, pushed aside the white curtains and looked out. Outside was a tiny balcony, only large enough to fit one person standing with any comfort, or perhaps two if they were very fond of each other. I had not noticed it the night before. I opened the window and a breeze blew into the room, carrying with it the slight refreshing chill of early morning. After hesitating for a moment I went back to my bed, removed the top blanket and wrapped it around myself, then stepped back over the sill onto the balcony. Below, the street lamps made little golden pools of light on the pavement. We were on the seventh floor of our hotel, and looked out over the tops of the surrounding buildings. I wondered what they all were, who lived there, what it was like to live in a city where so much of history had been made. But then the sun began to rise, and I forgot everything else in breathless awe. The stones of the city themselves seemed to absorb the light until they glowed from within, while in the distance a tiny wisp of pink cloud hung in the blue morning sky. For some time I could do nothing but stare. Then, prompted by some urge I could not name, I raised my hand and blew a kiss, out, beyond. To what? To Florence, to life, to beauty, to all those and more. An old, forgotten memory came back to me, of when I was a little girl, just after my parents had died. I used to wake up in the nights, alone in the big room at my grandmother's house, run to the window and blow kisses from it to God, thinking that perhaps, like me, he might be lonely.

Gloria found me there perhaps an hour or so later, still staring out over the city.

"It's wonderful, isn't it?" she said, squeezing out onto the tiny balcony to stand beside me. "Look, there. You can just see the river."

We were still looking and pointing and planning out the day when we heard a knock on the door. It was Mrs. Whildon.

She looked anxious. Her fingers were never still as she fidgeted with the canary yellow fringe on her sleeve.

"Girls," she said. "I've come to tell you that we're leaving tomorrow for France."

We stared at her incredulously. What would become of all our carefully laid plans? Finally Gloria spoke, just two words.

"What? Why?"

"Nice is close to the border," Mrs. Whildon went on, as if she had not heard. "It's a very international city, they say, and right by the ocean. You'd like that."

"But why?" Gloria was obviously beginning to lose patience with her chaperone.

Mrs. Whildon stopped fidgeting and her hands went rigid in her lap, but she spoke quietly.

"What do you know about the political situation in Europe?"

Gloria was silenced. I felt a pang of remorse for my ignorance. Mrs. Whildon continued in the same quiet voice.

"Our little friend Adolf Hitler has apparently taken it into his head to form a sort of German empire. Rumour has it that he plans to invade Poland. Germany and Italy have an alliance. If Poland is invaded Britain at least will declare war, in which case Italy could begin to be unsafe for English-speakers." Her voice took on a lighter, conciliatory note. "It is a shame that we will have to rush our time here and miss Venice, but we'll take more time in France and see more of the countryside." She got up. "Now get dressed. I think we will all want to make the most of this last day."

Gloria and I dressed in silence, still mentally digesting the news. When we went downstairs a few minutes later to meet the others we found Mrs. Beaufort in a state of near panic. The political situation was not drastically worse than it had been the day before, but the discussion of it had put her entirely beyond reason. Mr. Beaufort and Mrs. Whildon tried to soothe her while Mr. Whildon stood nearby, looking helpless.

"What are you saying, Beaufort? You bought railway tickets to France! No, no, we must take the first boat home."

Gloria and I exchanged glances of despair.

"Oh no," said Mrs. Whildon calmly, "you wouldn't want to cut your trip short like that. The danger isn't so great. In France we'll be fine."

Mrs. Beaufort gripped Mrs. Whildon's arm with one hand and her husband's with the other, protesting repeatedly, but she eventually became calm enough to accept the French scheme, though she could not be persuaded to go out with us that day and instead retired to her room leaning on Mr. Beaufort's arm.

Left in the lobby with Gloria and the Whildons, I stood uncertainly in the middle of the floor, feeling as if I ought to do something: join the British army to fight the Germans, run to Poland to stop the invasion, or stay with Mrs. Beaufort in her room all day. All were impossible notions except the last, and that, I reflected, would fit the least with my current state of mind.

"Come on Anna." Gloria plucked at my elbow. "If we only have one more day I don't want to spend it moping here. Let's get out!"

No idea could have been more welcome to me at that moment. It spared me any further thoughts of painful duty or guilty avoidance. Of course going with Gloria was the only thing to do. Surely she needed me as much as Mrs. Beaufort could.

I think we intended to lose ourselves. Without a word on either side we set off down the first side street that came to hand, after a while taking a turning, and then another, until we found ourselves on the edge of an open piazza. A market was going on, and the noises and sights and smells bombarded our senses at once. To our right, a little apart from the rest of the crowd, a little knot of people stood, clearly absorbed in something we could not see. Curious, we moved closer until we saw, in the centre of the group, a man sitting at an easel, painting. In front of him, sitting very still, was an old, white-haired couple, and behind him were several paintings on display. Most were small portraits, not masterpieces, but with a certain charm about them. A few were not of people at all, but of olive groves or views of the hills. One was of a small but powerfully built man in a military uniform. It was in the centre, as if the artist took particular pride in it. I was not a connoisseur of art, but I could see that his pride was justified. There was strength and purpose in the figure, a sense of arrested movement. The man's eyes held a fierce light. He lived.

We watched until the man had finished his work. Then I turned to go, but Gloria took hold of my arm and pulled me back.

"Anna," she said. "I want to get my portrait done. I haven't bought a single thing to remember Florence by, and this would be perfect. Better still, we'll both do it and then you can take mine home with you and I'll take yours so we'll have something to remember each other by."

Acknowledging this idea with a nod and a smile, I turned back with her to where the artist sat. The group of onlookers was gone, and he was busily cleaning his brushes and rearranging his things. He looked up as we approached.

"English?" he queried, raising one eyebrow.

Gloria and I looked at each other, then back at the artist. "American."

His eyebrow resumed its usual position and he nodded. It was clear that he was unimpressed by our heritage, but that business was business. Vaguely, I wondered what his reaction would have been if we had said that we were English.

"You wish to be painted?" He pronounced his English very carefully, emphasising each word. His tone and air were impersonal, professional, uninterested. He might have been thinking of painting two stone figures.

"Yes." Gloria was eager. "We both do." She immediately took her seat. "You don't mind if I go first, do you Anna?"

"No," I said. "Of course not. I'll go look at the market for a little while I wait. I'd like to find a present to take home for Grandmother."

As I walked away, I could hear the voice of the artist saying, "Turn your head more, like this. Yes, there."

I wandered through the market at a leisurely pace, enjoying the sights and smells, the glint of silver and the scent of leather, the fruit and flowers, and wondering what I should buy to take back to my grandmother. The urge to spend my money soon left me, however, and I began to think that I would buy her something in France, or England. The only thought that had any lasting hold on my mind was, *We're leaving tomorrow, and we've hardly even been here.*

At length I came back to where I had started and found Gloria sitting where I had left her while the artist put the finishing touches to her portrait.

When he was finished he held it at arm's length, looked at it critically, shrugged, and handed it to Gloria. "You are pleased?"

She looked at it for a moment, then nodded. "Oh, yes, thank you very much."

I moved to look at it over her shoulder. It was a very correct portrait. Every feature had been captured. The colouring and expression of Gloria's face were true to life. Every curl of the beautiful hair was done to perfection. Yet it lacked something, some nuance that I with my untrained eyes could not identify. I could only see that it held no life. The eyes were dull and empty, quite the opposite of both the real Gloria and the vibrant, living portrait of the man in military uniform.

I said nothing. Gloria had not expected a masterpiece. Neither had I, yet somehow I felt nettled. Was there a hint of something like deliberate intent in the lifeless eyes of Gloria's portrait, a touch of mockery in the eyes of the artist as he watched us? If there was it was gone at once, hidden beneath the former unreadable expression, and I mentally berated myself for being so unreasonably suspicious.

Yet I still had no desire to have my own portrait painted.

"But you must, Anna," remonstrated Gloria. "I did it, and now you must. Remember our agreement?"

I nodded, suddenly feeling incredibly tired, and sat in the place Gloria had vacated for me.

"Now I'll go have a look at the market," she said. "I'm getting a little hungry. Maybe I'll buy us some lunch."

She was gone. The artist worked in silence. Behind me the bustle of the market went on, but I hardly noticed it. My eyes had again been drawn to the paintings on display, and my mind was at work with curiosity to know who their subjects were, particularly the figure in the central portrait. Finally, gathering up my courage, I asked the artist.

"Who is the man in the portrait? The one in the middle."

The man paused in his work and looked around, though he obviously knew which portrait I meant, and he bowed his head. Then he turned back to me, and his face was no longer indifferent.

"He is *Il Duce,* our Great Leader, Mussolini," he said. "I painted that portrait years ago, before he became *Il Duce.* Don't speak, I paint your mouth. Ah, he is a great man. Even then you could see that he was a born leader. With a man like him to guide us, it may be possible for us to recreate the glory of the Roman empire." His eyes were bright with images, as if he saw the brilliant future spread before him. "Perhaps even to surpass it."

"I hope it will." I spoke out of sympathy with the vision in his eyes, without thought for what the consequences might be for the rest of the world if the ambitions of ancient Rome were brought to life again in the Twentieth Century.

He looked at me sharply. "You are American, you said?"

"Yes."

"Ah." He gave no explanation for his question, but continued painting in silence for a few minutes, then asked, "You speak Italian?"

"No," I answered sadly, "I only know a few words and phrases."

"Hmm." He was lost in concentration again.

It was not long before Gloria returned bearing some bread, cheese, and fruit, as well as a bundle of fresh daffodils.

"They were so beautiful," she said. "I couldn't resist. We can enjoy their brightness for the rest of the day." She pulled one out from the rest and tucked it behind her ear. Then she took out another for me.

"You won't mind the daffodil, will you sir?" she asked, looking at the artist.

"No, no, I have just finished," he said, and he handed me the portrait. Gloria looked over my shoulder.

"Anna, it's beautiful," she said. "It's better than mine, I think, though I can't exactly tell what it is that makes it better."

I could. He had painted life into me, perhaps because of my small offering of interest and sympathy; perhaps only for some whim of his own. For whatever reason, it was there. I was pleased and surprised, and thanked him with a smile, but it was only later, when

Gloria and I had returned to the hotel and were preparing for bed, that I noticed something else about it.

On the back, written in Italian and English, he had put a title for the painting, along with the date and his signature. The title read, *Una Cittadina del Nulla, A Citizen of Nowhere*.

* * *

The next day brought reality. We were leaving Italy because Mussolini, the same "Great Leader" I had been in awe of the day before, had allied himself with Hitler. The "Great Nation" I had supported the idea of only yesterday was to be made of the seized land of other nations and the blood of their people. I was ashamed of myself, and could only be glad that Gloria had not been present to hear me express hopes which now seemed foolish at best and treacherous at worst.

Yet the excitement of fleeing the country, even if there was no immediate danger, had its own charm. Gloria and I both took on the role of refugee with far more zealous feelings than I'm sure any true bearer of that title ever experienced. Ours was the feverish excitement of those who have heard the tiger's roar in the distance but have not yet felt its teeth.

We took the train from Florence early in the morning, when the world was lit only by the dim grey light before the dawn. Thus we left Italy behind us.

5

Our time in France remains a blur in my memory. On my Grandmother's recommendation I had faithfully kept a diary throughout our time in Italy, but after we left Florence I began to relax in my discipline, and the few entries I did bother to write conveyed little beyond, *Visited such-and-such museum today, very pretty. Gloria bought a hat.* Perhaps, had I mentioned that the hat was green, or that the guide at the museum had a big nose, it would act as a trigger to my memory and present the past with more clarity and colour. Perhaps that time only seems dim because its small doings were completely eclipsed by what came later.

What does appear in my mind is a sort of collage. I remember walks with Gloria along the Promenade des Anglaise in Nice, where we would stay for hours looking out to sea. I remember the vibrancy of the French countryside, the smell of lavender, crusty bread fresh from a bakery in a village in Provence, and strolling through the streets of Paris, the city where people never hurry if they can help it.

We lingered in Paris for some time, until Gloria and I almost began to feel as if we lived there. We had our favourite haunts, our morning ceremony of coffee and pastry consumption at a particular cafe near our hotel, and our afternoon routines of walking, driving, writing letters, or lounging on benches watching the people pass by. As long as we limited our conversation to single words, simple phrases, "Merci" "Bonjour", and the like, the Parisians ceased to regard us as though we had "Tourist" tattooed on our foreheads in block letters. They thought us unusually quiet mademoiselles, I'm sure, but they accepted our presence without comment. The housekeepers and bellboys at our hotel greeted us by name, and they would often gather in the evenings to hear Gloria play the piano in the dining room, while I stood by to turn her pages.

The Whildons and the Beauforts left us mostly to our own devices, and spent the greater part of their time in Paris resting from the rigours of travelling, though Mr. Beaufort found plenty of time and energy to examine architecture and make estimates, while Mrs. Beaufort admired jewellery to her heart's content. The Whildons too found time for their own particular pleasures, and we all enjoyed ourselves about equally in our different ways. That time seems quite idyllic in my memory. If I had any thoughts of impending disaster, any lingering idea that the thing which had caused us to leave Italy could find us on the streets of Paris, I ignored it, denying its existence as long as possible, until at last the day came when it could be ignored no longer.

Compared with the pleasantly hazy images of the weeks preceding it, September the first, 1939 stands out in my mind with striking clarity. We had all assembled in the hotel dining room for coffee in the late morning, as we often did, and Gloria played. I remember she played Chopin's Nocturne in E minor. There were a few other guests there as well -- an old lady, a middle-aged man, and a young girl. I remember that the man slurped his coffee.

It was Ansel, one of the boys who did the hotel's fetching and carrying, who brought the news. He came running in from the street, flushed with excitement, waving his arms and speaking very quickly in French. My French had improved during our stay there, but not enough for me to understand Ansel's words as they tumbled over each other in their hurry to escape his lips. Everyone in the room jumped up from their seats and followed him out to the street door, I along with the rest, though I understood nothing of the confused babel that ensued.

"Hitler has invaded Poland. France and Britain are expected to declare war within the week."

It was a woman's voice, coming from just behind me, and I turned to see one of the housekeepers. I never knew her name. She looked incredibly weary, but her voice was resigned as she translated the terrible news for me.

"I lost my husband in the Great War," she said, "and now I shall lose my two sons."

It was her horrible sense of inevitability that struck fear into me. It was then, for the first time, that I realised that this terrible thing, this war, was really beginning, and that people were not ready for it. Not so soon. Not again. I never saw that woman again, but I often thought of her. Over the next five years the pictures in my imagination varied a great deal, but through them all ran the thought of that woman and her two sons. For me they became symbols of the war, and in my mind the fate of the world rested on the shoulders of two young men I had never seen. In hopeful moments I saw them triumphant, winning the fight, ready to go home and tell their mother to look at them, to see that they were not dead -- but in moments of fear and despair I saw them dead or dying, while at home she called for them and they did not come.

It had happened, and again we were packing, seeking transportation to a safer location. Only this time, instead of insisting on being taken home immediately, Mrs. Beaufort refused to set foot on a boat crossing the Atlantic. Now that war was really being declared, her imagination ran wild thinking of German submarines attacking passenger ships, of the French or British mistaking us for Germans and sinking us, and countless other irrational and unlikely possibilities. The Whildons, who were really very concerned at the prospect of becoming caught up in a war far from home, tried to reason with her, but it proved useless. Mrs. Beaufort, always a willing victim of her fears, was absolutely unyielding. She *would not* travel home across the ocean, and it was clear that with their efforts to keep her reasonable even the nerves of the patient Whildons were beginning to fray, while Mr. Beaufort had given up completely and returned to his coffee in silence. I often wondered why the Whildons did not leave then and return themselves with Gloria. They were not bound to us. We had all agreed that if it seemed better to separate we would do so without bitterness on either side. I can only assume it was pity which kept them with us. Between my youth and timidity, Mrs. Beaufort's irrational panic, and Mr. Beaufort's uncertainty, we were a pretty group of helpless tourists to be wandering about what would soon become a war zone.

Looking back, the events of that day are almost comical, and in our surprise at this not-so-sudden plunge into war there is more than a hint of melodrama. Had it not been looming on the horizon for months, no, longer -- years? But it seems that people are often most blind to the thing immediately before them, be it good or bad. A girl will doubt the voice of the man she loves simply because it is "too good to be true", and I once heard of a man who claimed he still felt the fingers of the hand he had lost ten years before. Hope and fear are both capable of blindness.

Prime Minister Chamberlain of Britain had voiced the opinion of many less than a year before when he asked why we should trouble ourselves over "a quarrel in a faraway country between people of whom we know nothing". The European powers had tried to force peace, but peace is not forced. They sliced Czechoslovakia into pieces as if it were a choice bit of confectionery in an attempt to pacify Hitler, but things had gone too far to be stopped. The "quarrel in a faraway country" had come all too close, and would come closer.

That night my dreams were a confused jumble of faces, colours, loud noises and shouts. The next morning we left for England. The day after, war was officially declared.

Melanie Rose

Ashford

6

England, the lush green land which would come to mean so much to me, did not at first seem much of a haven. It was a temporary sanctuary, a small island nation to which we fled for a time, and would probably leave before long to seek another refuge. We sought the sense of safety given by a narrow channel of water as a substitute, because Mrs. Beaufort's fears prevented us from putting an entire ocean between ourselves and danger.

Thus it was with a somewhat disgruntled state of mind that I saw the city of London for the first time and realised that though I had resented being hustled onto a boat to get there I could not dislike it. It lacked the grandeur of Rome and the warm glow of Florence, and it did possess the careless beauty of Paris, but it had a certain magic of its own.

There the pattern of our travels changed, for after a short sojourn at a small hotel in North London, we received, in answer to letters from the Beauforts and myself informing her of our situation, a note from my grandmother. In it she expressed her sympathy for the plight in which we found ourselves, and enclosed a check for a rather substantial sum of money to be used for my maintenance during our extended stay, with a promise of more should it be needed. It was a very correct letter, very polite and even kind, but I, knowing my grandmother as I did, could see her pursed lips and the lines of disapproval crossing her forehead as she wrote of our "regrettable circumstances". In a separate letter addressed to me she gave greater vent to her feelings and expressed extreme disapproval at our decision to remain in Europe as well as her disgust at Mrs. Beaufort's irrational fears.

"Of course I don't blame you for that foolish woman's actions, Anna," she wrote. "However, if the opportunity does come at any time when you could persuade her to set foot on a boat, I urge you to take full advantage of it. If Mr. Beaufort had more backbone he would have insisted on her going and you would all be on your way home now. Even England may not be safe for long."

She then went on to tell me that an old acquaintance from her younger days, a widowed Mrs. Creeley, might still be living in London.

"It has been a few years since I heard from her, but we used to keep up a fairly steady correspondence. The last letter came shortly after her husband died. He left her with a fairly substantial income and a large empty house. If her situation is the same as it was then she may be willing to take you in for a while. Of course you will pay your own expenses. I do not ask you to live on her charity, but that sort of arrangement has the potential to be more comfortable than a hotel, and more economical."

At the bottom of the letter she had written Mrs. Creeley's address.

I communicated the greater part of this letter to Mr. and Mrs. Beaufort and it was agreed that we should seek out Mrs. Creeley's house the next afternoon in an attempt to discover if she still lived there and was in a position to welcome our temporary residence. Mr. and Mrs. Beaufort wanted to read the letter for themselves, and were rather offended for a time that I persisted in my denial. It did not seem to occur to them that I might wish to keep at least some of the contents of a private letter from my grandmother to myself. I might have yielded simply to avoid an argument if not for a few choice phrases which kept echoing in my head. In the end "that foolish woman's actions" and "if Mr. Beaufort had more backbone", as well as several other less-than-flattering statements, kept me firm in my resolve, and at last the Beauforts gave up their attacks, satisfying themselves instead with visiting the British Museum, jotting down many notes, buying several new notebooks and little gold pens with British flags on them, and eating a substantial lunch at a pub near our hotel.

I, feeling much better than I'm sure I was intended to feel at being left behind, sought out Gloria in our room and we dedicated the rest of the day to our own enjoyment. The Whildons were taking a boat to Greenwich for the afternoon, and we agreed that Gloria and I would walk them to the pier and continue our own adventures from there with the intention of meeting their boat again when it returned. A space of three hours was ours to enjoy as we chose, and for two healthy, energetic young women central London is an ideal place to spend one or many long afternoons. We first satisfied our taste for art with a visit to the National Gallery, and paid our tribute of awe with suitable deference to the lions in Trafalgar Square, which looked down on us with solemn dignity in spite of several parties of visitors who clambered about on their backs in flagrant disrespect.

In the last hour we wandered down to St. Paul's Cathedral. A service was just ending, and strains of music came down to us from the open doors as the choir finished. We mounted the steps and entered as those who had attended the service were leaving. Many were young men in crisp new uniforms, looking like toy soldiers just brought out of the box -- shiny little playthings ready to be lined up in neat rows and then knocked down again for the entertainment of some merciless child.

Silence descended as we entered. A few lingering groups stood here and there in the nave, but if they spoke at all it was only in whispers. Gloria and I did not speak, but moved as one to stand beneath the centre of the dome and look about us. It was a place for whispers or song, not for common jargon.

"Oh, Beaufort! Look at the dome! Do you think they sell miniatures?" Familiar laughter followed this remark, and Gloria and I did not need to turn our heads to know who had just entered the cathedral.

Exchanging pained looks, we looked around for some way of escape. The mood of reverent awe we had been enjoying was gone. The last thing I wanted was to be seen by the Beauforts at that moment, yet I was angry with myself. It did not seem right that reverence should be so easily replaced by annoyance, just because of a few silly words and a laugh.

To our right was an open doorway, and beyond a stairway going up. I touched Gloria's shoulder and pointed to it. She nodded and we ducked through the arch and began climbing. The stone steps curved up and up, higher and higher, until we emerged into a circular gallery which ran around the inside of the dome. Looking down, we could see to the floor of the cathedral -- a new and different view which almost made me dizzy with awe. From that height we found ourselves looking down at the tops of the Beauforts' heads. We could hear their voices coming up to us, echoing around the sides of the dome -- incoherent exclamations accompanied by hand gestures and nods of the head. Mr. Beaufort's bald spot shone with a truly amazing sheen from such a distance. They were gradually making their way toward the doorway which led to the stair we had taken, and we began looking about for somewhere else to go should they decide to visit the upper regions.

It was not long before we discovered another, smaller stairway, curving up as if to ascend the side of the dome itself. We set our feet to climbing, and before long came out into a smaller, outer gallery set at the top of the dome, with a splendid view over the city. Another stair led even higher, and so it went on, the steps always getting narrower and steeper, until we came to the last gallery of all, at the very top, and could go no further. This gallery was so small that no more than five people could have fit around inside it comfortably. A gilded railing encircled us. Below was the city of London, spread out like the most detailed map ever made. The broad, winding line of the Thames, the streets and squares, as well as the tiniest back streets and alleyways -- all were open to our view. In the years to come, I carried that view of London in my head, folded up and tucked away in a back corner, ready to be taken out and referred to at any time, growing more beautiful in memory until every rooftop appeared to my mind's eye as gilded as the dome of St. Paul's itself.

We lingered there until a clock, tolling the hour in another part of the city, reminded us that it was time to meet the Whildons. We had been there nearly an hour, yet I descended the stairs with regret, feeling as if I had stepped, just for an instant, on the threshold of heaven, only to turn back at the last moment.

Melanie Rose

7

Mrs. Creeley proved to be a wizened old lady, no higher than my shoulder, with unusually large eyes and a very sharp nose. She looked suspiciously at us over her eyeglasses when her shy little granddaughter led us into her sitting room the next day, as if she suspected that we were in league with the Nazis.

"So this is what happens to lifelong friendships," she sniffed. "I haven't heard from dear Eleanor in years, and now she sends me three strangers to maintain, at a time when we shall probably all be Germans within a year, if we're not blown to bits by a bomb first."

I found myself wondering how this small, soured person could ever have been a friend of my tall, straight, dignified grandmother.

"We would do our very best not to inconvenience you, Ma'am," said Mr. Beaufort, with a reddening of the face which spread from his bald spot to the tip of his nose. "Financially we will be entirely responsible for ourselves. We might even be able to ease your burdens a little...help about the house..."

Mrs. Creeley stared at Mr. Beaufort as if his scarlet head were a personal affront to her.

"I am not in the habit of making guests work for their keep. Violet does well enough for me. Young people ought to be kept busy, otherwise who knows what kind of trouble they would get into." She looked at the girl with an expression of condescending affection, as if she were a pack pony which must be kept employed lest it start cribbing.

Mr. and Mrs. Beaufort looked offended. I could see them making motions to each other as if they meant to get up and leave immediately. Then I looked at Mrs. Creeley out of the corner of my eye and saw with surprise a strange look of amusement on her face, as if she were getting a great deal of quiet entertainment out of the Beauforts' discomfort. Seeing her battle-axe countenance relax was rather startling, but it also gave me a little hope. I did not care much for the prospect of living in this woman's house, where even the furniture seemed to take on the hollowed, pinched contours of its mistress' face, but neither did I want to see more of my grandmother's savings get swallowed by our hotel expenses.

"Perhaps I could help Violet with her work." I said it humbly, but I could not keep my mouth from twitching slightly, for the situation as a whole struck me as being oddly funny. "I am young, and will be quite idle if I'm not given something to do."

Mrs. Beaufort said, "Anna!" in a tone of shock, and, looking at her, I could hear what she was thinking almost as clearly as if she had spoken it. *We shall NOT debase ourselves before THIS WOMAN!* "This woman" was definitely being thought in capital letters. I could see them in her eyes.

Mrs. Creeley looked as if she knew perfectly well that she was being thought about in capitals, and seemed enormously pleased. Turning away from the Beauforts as if they and their opinions were of no consequence whatsoever, she turned to me, and in a very businesslike manner began describing my possible duties.

"You will help Violet with the shopping, of course," she said. "She has trouble with those thin arms carrying the things home. Also a bit of cooking and cleaning -- a few other things. I assume you *can* cook. I will have a list for you when you come. Will tomorrow be soon enough? You *can* afford to pay the bill at your hotel for one more night I suppose?"

She was looking at me, not at the Beauforts. I nodded. I didn't trust myself to speak. I had won my point, embarrassed and annoyed the Beauforts, and secured us lodging, all in ten minutes or less, and I wasn't quite sure how I had done it. I only knew that thanks to Mrs. Creeley I now felt like a beggar who had sold herself into slavery to escape being thrown into prison by an angry hotel manager.

* * *

"She sounds like an absolute beast of an old lady," was Gloria's emphatic remark when I described the scene to her that afternoon.

We had joined Gloria and the Whildons for lunch at a pub near the hotel, and during that meal our morning visit had been glossed over in a somewhat uncomfortable manner by Mrs. Beaufort in between bites of shepherd's pie. Gloria and I had left the table as soon as we could. I had been suffering through the meal, certain that some tragedy would occur before we got our chance to leave -- that Mrs. Creeley would arrive carrying a red-hot poker to brand me into her service; that the hotel manager would arrive with a policeman to lock me up; or that Mrs. Beaufort would choke on the gravy in her shepherd's pie. Somehow, the last possibility struck me as being less tragic than the first two, so long as it did not prove fatal. My patience with Mrs. Beaufort was wearing thin enough that even the action of her jaws as she ate --

a small, quick, circular motion -- was enough to aggravate me.

At last we were able to make our escape, and the afternoon found us in Kensington Gardens.

"She can't be a complete beast," I said, wondering as I spoke why I was defending her.

"Yes, she can," said Gloria. "Giving people the benefit of the doubt is one thing and being ridiculous is another."

Did she really think me ridiculous?

We walked in silence for a while, enjoying the summer perfection of the park. It was a grey day, but not chilly, though I could smell rain in the air, as if it intended to fall at any moment and was only waiting for some signal. At least I imagined that it was waiting for something -- some particular person to reach the safety of their front door -- some event to reach its conclusion -- or perhaps even that it waited with malicious amusement to catch someone out in the open.

It was my fascination with this train of thought which distracted me to such a degree that I forgot to look where I was going. I was just giving the rain a sort of face in my mind (it had to be a special kind of face, I decided, one that could be kind or cruel or mischievous) when I heard Gloria say my name, and looked up just in time to get a close-up view of the front of a man's tweed jacket before it came into contact with my nose. Hands raised me up by my elbows and a man's voice said, "Excuse me." I apologised for my lack of attention and stepped back, intending to make a hasty retreat behind a convenient hedge, but first I looked up -- and my eyes met those of Perry Bertram, my acquaintance from the train to Florence.

Astonished to see him there so unexpectedly, I stopped where I was, and, I am afraid, stared rather longer than was strictly polite. I was certain that he would not remember me. So much had happened since we had met on the train. A war had begun. Who thought of chance meetings on trains when there was a war to think of? Finally I collected myself and turned to follow Gloria, who had stopped a little way ahead to look back at me in surprise. I had barely turned to go, however, when I heard my name.

"Did you enjoy Florence?" he asked when I turned around. His voice sounded amused. "Strange that we should run into each other like this, isn't it? I hope you were not hurt in our collision."

He had surprised me again. I had not expected him to recall our meeting on the train at all, yet he had, and even seemed glad to meet me again. I was astounded, but pleased as well, and to such a genuine expression of friendliness and concern I could only reply in the same spirit.

"Nothing is damaged except my dignity." I said, laughing.

"I'm glad to hear it," he said. "I was lost in my thoughts and didn't look where I was going."

"That's all right." I said. "I wasn't paying as much attention as I should have been either." *Paying no attention at all would be more accurate,* I thought. I had been giving the rain a face and personality, but I didn't care to admit it.

A brief silence ensued, and I remembered Gloria. Cursing myself for my lack of manners, I called her over and introduced my acquaintance to her as, "Mr. Bertram. We met in the train on the way to Florence."

They shook hands.

"Perry will do," he said. "Your friend and I met under unique circumstances. She assisted me in the tedious work of trying to read an Italian newspaper. Formality is hardly necessary for such an acquaintance, and anyway, being called 'Mr. Bertram' makes me feel like my grandfather." He looked at me again then. "I have thought of you and your chaperones since then and wondered how you enjoyed your time on the continent, but I admit I expected that you would return to America when war was declared, if not before."

Fumblingly, because I feared appearing disloyal to Mr. and Mrs. Beaufort even if I wasn't feeling very charitable towards them, I said, "We are going to be staying in London with an old friend of my grandmother's. We understood that there was some doubt as to the safety of taking a boat home when a war was going on."

"Hm."

Gloria smoothly cut through the discomfort by inviting Perry back to the hotel for tea, but he excused himself.

"I'm afraid I'm already late," he said, looking at his watch. "My great-aunt is expecting me. She's a sharp old lady -- very keen on punctuality."

We both apologised for keeping him, and then we parted.

"You never told me about meeting him on the train," said Gloria, somewhat reproachfully, when we had begun walking again.

"I didn't know you would find it interesting," I replied, a little defensively, for the truth was I had held that memory sacred as the first time on our journey when I had felt truly free to be myself.

Gloria was not satisfied, however, until I had told her every detail of our meeting and conversation. I had never, since I had first known her, been reluctant to tell her anything, but when I had finished my story the memory seemed different since it had been shared, like opening a window on a sunny day shows up the dust on the furniture.

Ashford

8

We moved ourselves into Mrs. Creeley's house the following day. The Whildons, to my regret but not my surprise, began to discuss travel plans as soon as they heard we were leaving the hotel. They had only stayed out of kindness, and now that we had somewhere to go they considered their duty fulfilled. I could not blame them, but at the same time I bitterly regretted that they were to go, and that I would lose Gloria's companionship. With my friend gone, I could not look forward with much pleasure to life in Mrs. Creeley's house with the Beauforts. I had a sense that I would be spending a considerable amount of time keeping my chaperones and our hostess from each other's throats.

I was to share a room with Violet, and though she said nothing about it -- indeed she rarely spoke at all -- I got the impression that I was not a welcome addition to her life. She was a wispy little thing, a year or two younger than I was, with large blue eyes which were usually focused on something in the vicinity of the floorboards. I was fascinated by the relationship between Violet and Mrs. Creeley -- so different yet so similar to mine with my grandmother. Both women were strong-willed and somewhat controlling, but Mrs. Creeley's attitude toward Violet seemed to me like my grandmother's to me with the humanity taken out of it. It was the relationship between dog and master -- a curious mixture of affection and subjection.

Gloria came to help me unpack. We sat on the floor in my corner of the room, folding clothes and putting them away in the little chest of drawers which had been cleared to make room for me. The process took longer than perhaps it should have because now and then we would come across a relic of our travels together and would promptly be thrown into a fit of remembrances.

"Oh! That's the scarf you got in Nice, at that little place by the Promenade, when Mrs. Beaufort bought those dreadful engraved bracelets."

They truly had been dreadful, and Gloria and I, looking at them later, had discovered on the inside edge the inscription *Made in the USA*, which had set us laughing at the time just as it did now.

In the midst of our enjoyment Violet slipped into the room to sit quietly on the edge of her bed, staring blankly at the opposite wall. I, glancing at her just long enough to see that she seemed eager to be left alone, turned my attention back to Gloria.

"I wish you were not leaving so soon," I said. "I don't know what I'll do without you here to keep me company. Or else I wish I could go back with you."

"I wish I could stay," said Gloria. "You're going to be in the most exciting place. Anyway, it won't last that long. England and France won't let it, and the President's bound to come to his senses one of these days and realise that America's simply got to help, and then the war will be over in a snap. Nobody's ready for another long war. They'll put an end to it soon."

Would they? Would it really be over in a snap? We were both hopeful. But we had not experienced the Great War firsthand as our elders had, and I remembered the face of the French woman whose sons were going to war and wondered if our hopes were, after all, brittle and unrealistic.

A sudden commotion reached our ears from downstairs. Violet jumped up and rushed to the door, Gloria and I followed, and the three of us ran down the stairs and entered the sitting room together, tumbling through the door almost on top of each other.

Downstairs we found our elders and a visitor, all apparently absorbed in acting out a scene from an old drama -- with Mrs. Creeley performing the best interpretation I have ever seen of the old, battle-hardened warrior queen. Mrs. Beaufort took on the role of begging prisoner, the stranger (a tall, dark-haired young man) was the courageous knight, a defender of the weak, and Mr. Beaufort stood nearby, obviously waiting for the right moment to come in for the comic relief.

It took me several minutes to realise that Mrs. Creeley's cane was not a sceptre, that the visitor was not dressed in armour, but an airman's uniform, and that the matter they discussed was not Mrs. Beaufort's possible execution but merely the question of whether or not to install an Anderson shelter in the garden.

Mrs. Creeley was against it. She pursed her lips and her sharp eyes glittered indignantly. Mrs. Beaufort was obviously set on the idea, and I saw at a glance that her insistence was only strengthening our hostess's resolve. Mr. Beaufort stood by helplessly, clearly at a loss. The visitor had been saying something which neither I nor anyone else in the room could hear. Indeed it was difficult to hear any distinct part of the conversation because all three of the primary speakers were talking at once. Mrs. Creeley's voice alone carried enough force to be heard.

"I have already hired Samuel to dig up half the garden, and he will plant it to potatoes next spring. I refuse to fill up the rest with a hideous air-raid shelter. We have the corner of the cellar if necessary. In any case,

I am old. Who is there to worry if my life is cut short by a bomb a few months earlier than it would be otherwise?"

The visitor looked annoyed, as well he might.

"I'm not only thinking of you," he said, losing patience with her, "even though you are the picture of health and hardly likely to die of natural causes any sooner than the rest of us. I'm concerned about Violet as well. She is young, and if she chooses to stay with you against my advice, we would all wish at least that you both have some way of taking shelter in an emergency. And even if that consideration doesn't move you, surely you would not wish to endanger your guests."

"I do not keep them here by force," she replied waspishly. "They are free to leave whenever they choose, and your sister is under no obligation to stay, daughter of my dead son though she is. If she considers herself unsafe she may go stay with the Bertrams. I can still live by myself, old and infirm though I am."

Mr. and Mrs. Beaufort took advantage of the opportunity to leave the room, both looking extremely offended. Mrs. Creeley exited in the opposite direction. Gloria and I moved to the door more slowly. Nobody had taken any notice of us, except the stranger, Violet's brother, who acknowledged us with a nod and a disarming smile before turning back to look thoughtfully at his sister. I thought then that I would never have guessed their relationship. Violet's timidity formed a striking enough contrast to her brother's commanding air even without the physical differences, of which there were many. Yet, in the moment before we left the room, I looked back, and saw a look on Violet's face that startled me -- a determination which more than equalled her brother's. Stubborn brown eyes stared into equally stubborn blue ones.

"I'm not going, Tristan."

The brown eyes held for a moment, then withdrew.

"I know," said Tristan. "Damn your loyalty."

Melanie Rose

9

Violet did not leave, and neither did we. The Anderson shelter was not put in, though Mrs. Beaufort rarely missed an opportunity to drop a hint about it. The Whildons and Gloria departed, to my great sorrow, but life continued, and we began to establish a sort of routine again, holding tightly to the small tangible traditions of breakfast at eight and tea at four as our only hold on the security of past days.

For some time the expected bombing raids did not come, while Europe went through what became known as the "phoney war" and great men laid their plans and our airmen (including Violet's brother Tristan) dropped pamphlets over Germany. Through it all the rest of us waited on tenterhooks and scanned the newspapers for word of any change or development. Nerves were constantly frayed, gas masks kept close at all times. Inactive in body but weary in mind, we prepared for a "worst" which was slow in coming.

Gloria wrote to tell me that they had reached home without mishap, and we began a fairly steady correspondence. In all the activity which had taken place before her departure we had forgotten to exchange our portraits from Florence, and she cheerfully informed me that she took that as a good sign, that it meant that I must return home soon, if only to visit her at her home in Georgia and hand over the painting.

Winter came, and the days grew short and dreary. Snow fell from time to time, only to be washed away by the grey drizzle of rain which inevitably followed it. Christmas Eve arrived, and Violet and I were sent out to buy a chicken, our one Christmas luxury.

The two of us had established an understanding over the past months which, if not exactly friendly, was at least workable. I had felt a great deal of respect for her ever since the day she had decided to stay with Mrs. Creeley instead of seeking safety elsewhere, but this was coupled with a feeling of unease in her presence, for I could never tell what she was thinking. At the same time, she was the least demanding companion of those who were available to me, and once I got past the initial shyness her personality was refreshingly uncomplicated. She asked no unnecessary questions and met everything that came her way with a simple, straightforward attitude. A thing either was or it wasn't, it worked or it didn't, the answer was yes or no, never maybe. If Mrs. Creeley was on a rampage looking for clothespins (which had happened several times, not only with clothespins but also with window-shades, straight-pins and sundry items of clothing) and asked everyone in her accusatory fashion where they were, Mrs. Beaufort would spend twenty minutes explaining why she could not possibly know where they were, things were such a mess, she had not been the last to use them, etcetera. Violet would simply say no, she hadn't seen them, then leave the room to search the house and be back with the item required before Mrs. Beaufort had finished listing her excuses.

We found the chicken and I carried it under my arm wrapped in brown paper while Violet collected the rest of our groceries in a basket. We went on, stopping occasionally to reply to the Christmas greetings dropped by fellow shoppers, most of whom seemed in a very cheerful frame of mind as they balanced their

Christmas chickens and sacks of somewhat wilted greenery. It was Christmas, after all, their faces seemed to say, no bomb had yet fallen on us, and England would beat Germany, of course, because that was just the way things were.

A light drizzle began as we finished the shopping, and it picked up as we hurried home through the crowded streets. We were soaked through and shivering by the time we reached the front door of Mrs. Creeley's house, but on Christmas Eve even Mrs. Creeley was not too economical about the use of fuel. The house was warm to welcome us, a bundle of fresh holly lay on the table in the entrance hall, still spattered with raindrops, and on the rug in front of the fire in the sitting room stood Perry Bertram, drying out his coat.

A thought had passed through my mind some time before, when Mrs. Creeley had alluded to "the Bertrams" that perhaps the family she referred to and my acquaintance were related in some way, but time had passed with no further mention of that family and I had dismissed the idea as foolish. No doubt there were many Bertrams in the country, the relatives of Mrs. Creeley among them, and it was merely a strange coincidence that I had become somewhat acquainted with another who bore that name.

Perry greeted me with a friendly nod and smile.

"They were all just telling me that you were expected soon, and here you are. I seem to have a strange habit of meeting you at random and now it turns out we are attached to the same people. How delightfully strange that is. How are you Violet?" He approached to give his cousin an affectionate hug. His presence seemed to have had a calming effect on everyone in the room. It was strange to see Mrs. Beaufort and Mrs. Creeley smiling at the same time -- strange indeed to see Mrs. Creeley smiling at all as she did at this young man, in spite of the water still dripping from his coat onto the Persian rug which had been her mother's.

After the greetings had been exchanged Violet and I hauled the chicken, along with the rest of the groceries, into the kitchen. We could hear the sound of voices drifting in from the next room, along with the most cheerful laughter to be heard in that house for months. For once in perfect accord, we glanced at each other, hurriedly put the things away, and returned with speed to the sitting room -- to the firelight flitting over the walls -- to the unaccustomed warmth and laughter.

"It's lovely to have fresh holly from Ashford," Violet said to Perry later that evening, when we were all seated around the fire. Mrs. Beaufort's head was nodding, and Mr. Beaufort, who sat too near the fire, fanned his red face sleepily with the air of someone trying to frighten away a swarm of gnats. Mrs. Creeley still watched and listened, her sharp old eyes fixed on whoever was speaking at any particular moment. Her gnarled stick leaned against her chair, and in the shadows she looked like a witch from old legend, yet I was no longer afraid of her. I had heard her laugh, and I had seen the look of affection she gave Perry. No creature capable of love should be feared -- only loved in return and respected. It was something that both Violet and Perry had learned long ago. Love begets love, and even Violet's timid devotion and loyalty earned her affection of a sort, while Perry's less guarded feelings of regard for his great-aunt had clearly made him a favourite.

I had been drifting in my thoughts again, gazing vacantly at the fire, and earned a laugh from Perry.

"You've had that look on your face at least once every time I've seen you," he said, "like a seeress staring into the future and seeing the fate of the world. I hope your visions were happy ones."

Ashford

I laughed in return to shake off my thoughts.

"I'm just getting a little tired."

In truth I was a little sleepy. Better to say that than to retrace the winding journey my thoughts had taken.

In a rare moment of openness, Violet said quietly, "If I were a seeress I would be afraid to see the fate of the world today."

We all became a little solemn at that point. It was easy to forget for short moments the threat which shadowed all our lives, but it was always there in the background, waiting.

Perry left soon after that, saying he must return to Ashford that night. Violet and I walked with him to the door. The evening was growing dark and a light snow was falling. Perry said good-bye to both of us, then said more quietly to Violet.

"Tristan wrote to me about what happened before he left. If anything happens you are welcome at Ashford -- all of you." The last words were directed at me as well. "I hope you can convince Aunt to come. London may not be safe for much longer. We have two refugee children from Poland in the house at the moment, and Jerry and Mum and Dad and Grandma are all there, but we can always manage a few more."

He waved his hat at us and left the house. I found myself looking at the bunch of holly on the side table -- bright, festive spots of red berries against dark green leaves, lighting up the dim hall.

"We should put it up in bunches all over the house," said Violet suddenly. "It will help it feel like Christmas tomorrow."

Melanie Rose

Ashford

10

Christmas passed uneventfully, set apart from other days only by the holly, the chicken, and a nameless aura which, for one day, kept peace in the house. For that day Mrs. Creeley and Mrs. Beaufort avoided sharp words, though they came near it several times, and the atmosphere was easy and tranquil, if not exactly festive or buoyant.

In the months that followed Violet and I grew more comfortable with each other and though she remained a mystery to me I came to like her better than ever. I especially loved the stories she told me about Ashford. It seemed so separate from London, set apart by itself in the wooded hills of Devonshire. From Violet's descriptions I could see the old, rambling house with its odd angles, sloping slate roofs and the high, ivy-covered stone walls of its garden filled with sweet-smelling flowers: roses and lavender, lilac, and one old knotted wisteria in the corner. From her stories, I gained a misty view of the family there, as if I were seeing them through a light rain. There was Perry's grandmother, the matriarch, warm and calm, "as if" said Violet "she carried the sunlight with her" as different from her sister Mrs. Creeley as could be, except for a certain stubborn streak which was a family characteristic and in this case had resulted in a ban on the use of electric lights at Ashford. There was Perry's beautiful, absentminded mother, flitting about the house on noiseless feet, as silent and graceful as the gauzy dresses she always wore. Mr. Bertram, an older version of

Perry, had a passion for scholarship, an interest in cultivating rare herbs, and an extreme compassion for anything hurt or helpless, which led not only to the addition of occasional homeless waifs (and refugee children) to the household, but also to the transformation of one corner of the garden into a sort of hospital for injured creatures in various stages of recovery. Perry's younger brother Jerry was their father's special care. Violet described Jerry as "both slow and quick at once, as if part of his mind were missing but the loss only made the rest sharper". The two refugee children and the English sheepdog Mopsy rounded out the household, but Violet had not been to Ashford since the children's arrival, and could not put portraits of them in my head with her descriptions.

"There's always a lovely smell about it too," Violet said one day as we ironed shirts and linens together. "Something like this," she held a freshly pressed tablecloth to my nose "and like freshly baked bread, and herbs from the garden, with a little bit of Aunt Lilly's perfume mixed in. It really isn't very nice perfume," she added "but it all combines to make the Ashford smell, and that's perfect."

It was in these conversations as well that I learned what I had wondered before but would never have asked, that Violet was an orphan as I was. Her father had been Mrs. Creeley's only child. Neither of her parents had had very good health, partially due to their residence in a coal-mining town where the black fragments rarely left the air clear for long, and they died within two years of each other when Violet and Tristan were very young. The brother and sister had grown up at Ashford in the care of their relatives, until Mrs. Creeley's husband had died, when she asked for Violet to come live with her. I guessed that Violet had come out of a sense of duty as well as out of pity for her grandmother, else I could not see her leaving a place that she still spoke of with such affection and longing. But duty and pity, I guessed, had been the driving forces of Violet's life for some time.

So the winter passed, and the phoney war continued -- a time of strained nerves, of expectations never fulfilled, and constant anticipation of terror or triumph. We had so much to fear and nothing to do but sit and wait for our fears to be fulfilled, or not. We listened for the warning sirens -- heard them echo in our sleep -- but nothing happened. Tristan wrote to Violet of missions over Germany and the smell of danger. Violet would read me his letters sometimes and we both envied him his position of action.

The news from Europe grew worse. America remained officially neutral. Gloria wrote letters describing the frustration of her two brothers and the unrest of the young set in her hometown who longed for action while their elders warned and fretted and advised caution.

An air of frustration permeated the house. The source of our restlessness was rarely named, but it was always there lingering around the corner in the hall or up the stairs. Mrs. Creeley found release by ordering Violet and me to rearrange the household furniture repeatedly, move that chair against the wall, take that table upstairs, turn the carpet the other way. Mrs. Beaufort in her turn objected to the changes and expressed her feelings to her husband, and sometimes to me, often purposely in the hearing of our hostess, which only served to intensify the animosity already existing between them. Violet avoided everyone, including me, though I hope I do not exaggerate in saying that she was less eager to avoid my company than that of others. As usual her manners were incredibly difficult to read, but I think I may safely say that she was not usually averse to my company, even if she did not necessarily welcome it or initiate contact. She was more content with solitude than any human creature

I have met, before or since. Mrs. Beaufort, even at her most peevish, required the company of somebody at all times. I think she would willingly have endured several hours with only Mrs. Creeley for company rather than one completely alone. From glimpses I caught of Violet from time to time, I guessed that her fertile mind needed little or no outside stimulation. She was almost completely self-sufficient, most at ease in a task she could complete herself, accepting assistance if it was offered yet never seeking it. The only people I ever saw her completely at ease with were her brother Tristan and her cousin, Perry.

Perry came to see us from time to time throughout that year, when he came to London on business, and for an afternoon or so the mood of the house would lift, as if he brought the comfort and fresh air of Ashford with him, along with bits of news (his father had found a young fox with a broken leg, his grandmother had at last given in to electricity for the sake of hearing the radio reports). I believe Violet and I both lived a sort of second life at Ashford in our minds, a life where it was always spring and the sun always shone over the walled garden of that lovely house. In this I envied Violet, for her second life could be fed with numerous memories of the real place -- mine could only be imaginary.

Everyone enjoyed Perry's visits. Mr. Beaufort welcomed him as another representative of the male gender, and monopolised a great deal of his time by cornering him in the stairwell to discuss the grave masculine topics of war, mayhem, and machinery. If Mrs. Beaufort waxed too eloquent at dinner on the subjects of dress or the importance of a balanced diet, Mr. Beaufort relieved his feelings by winking covertly at Perry and giving vent to a jocular chuckle which escaped nobody and annoyed everyone.

Mrs. Creeley was constantly at work to convince Perry to stay longer, and many were her methods, both open and secret, of achieving that end.

"I really think she'd stoop to anything to keep him," I laughed to Violet one evening. Perry had just left to return to Ashford, and Mrs. Creeley had vented her frustration and disappointment by another rampage. "I hope he parks his car out of the way. I wouldn't be surprised if she tried to disable it."

"There he's safe," said Violet, though she smiled at the picture my remark suggested. "Perry never drives. He always takes the train and walks from the station."

I thought then that I should have noticed that Perry did not drive, but I had never thought of it. Mrs. Creeley's house was a long walk from the train station, and Violet had mentioned before that the family at Ashford had a car (it was one of Mr. Bertram's pet projects) so I had put two and two together and mistakenly arrived at six.

It was not long after my talk with Violet that the subject of Perry came up between Mr. and Mrs. Beaufort. It was in the afternoon of a day in early March, and the three of us were in the sitting room. Violet and I had been keeping ourselves busy with Red Cross work and I was hemming a shirt for the cause -- not with ease, for I had only recently learned the trick of it, and my attention was almost entirely focused on keeping the stitches straight and not pricking my fingers. Perhaps because I sat so quietly in the corner and did not look up, or perhaps because it was just their habit, Mr. and Mrs. Beaufort spoke without reserve. At first I did not heed their conversation at all, for my mind was on other things, but after a time their talk, from its place as a babel on the edge of my consciousness, began to filter through and make itself interesting to me.

"Oh, I agree that he's a very pleasing young man," Mrs. Beaufort was saying, "and his company certainly provides some much-needed variety around here, but doesn't it seem like there must be something just a little...well...wrong?"

"I can see nothing, my dear, unless perhaps the shortness of his visits. It has been very pleasant to me to have the society of a young man -- makes me feel quite young again myself." I heard Mr. Beaufort squelch back into his chair with a contented chuckle and unfold the newspaper, and I looked up just in time to see Mrs. Beaufort send him a supremely annoyed look.

"Really Beaufort!" she said, "I married you thirty years ago for your rakish good looks, but sometimes I wonder if there was ever a brain to back them. No, what I meant was--"

I lost track of the conversation for a moment in trying to picture a young Mr. Beaufort with rakish good looks, but soon gave up and fell to listening again.

"--the only young man of his age we see who isn't in uniform and dashing off to fight somewhere. I would hate to accuse someone we all like so much of cowardice, but it all smells rather fishy to me. In a time like this when everyone has to do their part -- and we've all heard of these pro-Germans they say are all over the country--"

I pricked my finger. A drop of blood fell onto the clean white shirt I was hemming. I put my finger in my mouth and took the shirt away to the kitchen to try to remove the stain. It would not do to send an already bloodstained shirt out to some poor soldier who waited in the trenches for a clean one. I did not want to hear the rest of the conversation. That our friend was pro-German I refused to believe. I did not want to think of Perry as a coward, but what proof did I have that he was not, and truly, who could blame him if he was? I did not want to let Mrs. Beaufort's speculations effect my thoughts, yet subtly they did. We were all so very desperate about the war. It was in everybody's thoughts and on everybody's lips. Our boys were our heroes and we cheered and hoped and grieved for them. There was something shameful in leaving the fighting to others. It was the act of a coward, a shirker.

I shook myself and said that I would not think of it, that it was Mrs. Beaufort's idle chatter only and there was probably no truth in it. Violet came in and I showed her the bloodstain and we laughed at my sewing and my pricked fingers. I thought of asking her about Perry, but how to phrase it? I changed my mind. There was no kind or tactful way to say, "Is your cousin pro-German, or just a coward?" So I said nothing about it, and pushed the thought to the back of my mind, and things went on as before except for occasional moments when I felt it there, tickling at my consciousness as if it were the tiniest of splinters, invisible to common sight but persistently refusing to be pulled out.

Melanie Rose

11

The winter had seemed to pass slowly, but spring came at last, and all of London put on a brighter face for fair weather and a fresh start. Spring also brought new tasks to occupy our minds and bodies. Half of the garden was dug up and planted to potatoes and we all got a certain amount of satisfaction out of "doing our bit". Things were going badly on the mainland. Germany invaded Norway and Denmark and to us, sitting at home in London, there seemed to be nothing to stop them. We knew our soldiers were out there, fighting and working for Europe, for England, and for us, but we could not see them and their efforts and the enemy continued to move forward. Yet, in the spring, when the sun broke through the rain clouds occasionally and lit London's grey streets to silver, none of us could find it in our hearts to be too downcast. We kept our hands in the dirt, our minds on hemming shirts and digging potatoes, and felt that in that way we stood behind our boys.

The United States remained neutral, and we ground our teeth companionably over the faithlessness of allies, forgetting that three out of five of us would have called ourselves American, had we thought. Once, in early April, Mr. Beaufort ventured to suggest that catching a boat for home was still an option and didn't seem too dangerous at present, but silence was the only answer he received except for a pleading look from his wife which seemed to contain all her panic of months before as well as a little extra. No more mention was made of going home after that, and I, in spite of my Grandmother's advice to push for a journey should I see any opportunity, remained silent. To me it seemed that our lives had become involved in some disastrous chess game which was taking place in Europe, and until the game was played out we were nothing but pawns ruled by a few corrupt and scheming minds.

In May we heard that Chamberlain had resigned as Prime Minister and would be replaced by Churchill. Many people had been disappointed in Chamberlain for his reluctance to react to the Nazi threat, and most felt that the change was for the better. Mrs. Creeley alone in the household remained sceptical, saying that change was usually for the worse, better a fool you know than a fool you don't, and so on. The other news which reached us the same day was disheartening. Germany had invaded Holland, Belgium and Luxembourg. It was a matter of days before the Dutch army surrendered, a few weeks and the Belgians gave in, and it seemed as if the world would be swallowed up -- that before the year ended we would all be sent to concentration camps and tattooed with numbers.

* * *

Strangely enough, as our fears continued to grow, so did our feelings of security and comfort. Even though they were only brought on by the vague familiarity we were gaining of our new home and its surroundings, at least we were (for the most part) no longer dogged by fear of getting lost or falling into strange company. I knew my way around the part of the city in which Mrs. Creeley had her house very well by that spring and summer, and had begun, in my spare time, to venture greater distances into the city, sometimes with Violet as a sort of guide, but more often alone, wandering about in an aimless sort of way. I often felt that it had less to do with me getting to know London, and more to do with London getting to know me. The city seemed to have its own essence, a personality which reached out to some and repelled others. Mr. Beaufort found it "a city just like other cities, but wetter" but to me it had a vibrant sort of beauty which was only enhanced by wetness and showed to best advantage in its rain-washed streets, the light of its lamps shining through the mist, and the moist luminous green of its parks.

Spring passed and summer came. Violet and I had been given the task of watering and caring for the potatoes. I surprised myself with the discovery that I enjoyed digging in the moist earth, caring for the plants, and especially, when it came time to harvest them, pulling up the mature plants and discovering how the potatoes had flourished. I often found myself wondering how it was that potatoes were discovered to be edible. Were they found out by some poor starving wretch thousands of years ago? I had a sort of mental image of the discoverer of potatoes, who looked a little like an emaciated Churchill, sitting on the ground in rags, an uprooted potato plant in one hand, looking quizzically at the lumpy things hanging from the slender roots as if weighing the advantages of death by poison versus death by starvation.

The Germans moved their attack to France that summer, and London turned into a large, seething mass of indignation. Britain stepped immediately into the role of defensive sibling. She and France had had their arguments of course, but no one else should claim to torment one without the other stepping in. Tristan and his comrades were moved to a base in the French countryside to assist in the defence. "Our base is huge," he wrote to Violet. "It's not just us and the French. There are Americans here too -- rough fellows mostly, just looking for excitement, but it encourages us to see that there are some who are willing to come help us, even if it is only the mutineers and black sheep."

I also received a letter concerning the attack. It came from Gloria, expressing her outrage at the American government.

"Do you know," she wrote, "that the French government actually appealed directly for assistance, but we were 'unable to oblige'? It makes me quite envy you, with your Red Cross work and your potato planting, though I never thought I should envy *that*. At least you're able to *do* something. Mrs. Whildon has tried to organise some sort of local group to assist the cause, and I joined because I really *wanted* to help. We've had two meetings. Anna, our 'group' is made up of five old biddies, their knitting, and their gossiping tongues. The only suggestion they had was that we should knit stockings to send to the poor children in Belgium. I'm sure the poor things *need* stockings, but I wish there was something more we could do. I was all ready to get up a charity concert or go marching to Washington in protest, but my grey-haired companions apparently thought my ideas required too much energy and wanted nothing to do with them. Besides, I dare say anything else would cut in on their gossiping time."

In my reply I tried to pacify her, saying that being in London was rather more frightening that exciting, and that digging potatoes was quite as prosaic as ever, yet I could not deny that I greatly preferred my position to hers. I could not explain, to her or to myself, why exactly this was, but I found that it was true. I, who had always loved quiet and peace, and avoided upheaval, could not find more than a hint of desire in myself to leave the threatened turf of England and return home to America and security.

More often, as I walked through the city, I would see the train platforms crowded with refugees fleeing to the countryside, mostly children. Sometimes I gave them a little money, but I could not afford much, for what little I had came from my grandmother, and was sent at regular intervals so that I would not be a burden on Mrs. Creeley.

One rainy day in late May, as I was in the hall preparing to go in quest of groceries, I found myself unexpectedly accosted by Mrs. Beaufort.

"Ah, you are going out, my dear -- in this wet, and all alone?"

Violet had a bad cold and was staying in, so I replied that yes, I was.

"You'd better let me go with you, poor thing. All this rain! And how will you carry all the things and your umbrella too?"

Call me suspicious for attributing any other motive to Mrs. Beaufort's words than kindly concern for my welfare, but I had gone out alone countless times, in and out of the rain, and she had never expressed such concern before. However, I didn't think it would be quite polite to refuse her offer, so I said she was welcome to come if she really wished to, but that we should be leaving soon if we were to be back in time for our usual dinner hour.

"Of course. I'll only be a moment."

A "moment" is, of course, a poorly defined space of time, but it is generally supposed to be of short duration. Mrs. Beaufort's moment exceeded half an hour, and, as I had already laced myself into my boots and did not dare set foot on Mrs. Creeley's pristine carpets, I had to resort to pacing back and forth in front of the door while I waited.

I heard her as she moved throughout the house, telling her husband where she was going, inquiring about sundry items of clothing, and even opening the door of Violet's room to ask her where the second grocery basket was.

Finally she was ready, and we went out together into the pouring rain.

"At last," she gasped, when we had progressed several yards beyond the door. "I couldn't stand another moment in that house. Anna, I don't know how much more of this I can take. Sometimes I think that our hostess has no manners at all. I would hate to find fault with the locals in general, but surely we live with the worst of them all."

I could find no reply to give. It was true that Mrs. Creeley in a temper was a sight to behold. It was also true that she generally flew into a rage at least once a day. But she had not denied us a place when we had needed one most, and day after day I had seen, in the faces of the refugees, signs of trials and sufferings much greater than ours had ever been. It was the thing which often gave me patience to bear with Mrs. Creeley, and it was a thing which Mrs Beaufort, who had barely stirred a quarter of a mile from the house for the past three months, had not seen and could not understand until she did, if then.

She continued to vent her frustration for the rest of the walk. I said little, but little was required of me. She wanted only a listener. I felt oddly mature, as if our positions were reversed and I were the elder. I had never expected my chaperone to confide in me.

We purchased the groceries and turned for home. Almost without realising it I altered our course a fraction, and we passed by the train station.

I can attribute no particularly virtuous motive to my action. I was only tired of hearing her endless complaints and did the one thing I knew of which might possibly silence her. As to what other effect it would have, I confess I thought little enough about it.

The effect was much greater than I could have imagined. Mrs. Beaufort stopped in her tracks, staring at the women and children crowding the platform, then turned to me.

"Poor things!" she said, an angry flush spreading across her face. "Does nobody feed them?"

Before I knew what was happening she had rushed to the nearest huddled group and was handing out the groceries in her basket to the children in a frenzy, without stopping to consider whether raw beef would do much to benefit a child sleeping on an open train platform. Finally, at a loss for anything else to give them, she handed over her umbrella (which I'm sure was much more appreciated than the raw beef) and came scurrying back to the shelter of mine.

Our walk home was silent. When Mrs. Creeley complained about the absence of certain items from our basket Mrs. Beaufort, with unusual meekness, claimed forgetfulness, and I did not contradict her, though it earned us both a severe lecture.

Melanie Rose

12

A character such as Mrs. Beaufort's does not change overnight. Generally changes are small and easily overlooked, the virtues being nearly as abrasive as the vices and therefore somewhat difficult to distinguish.

In part Mrs. Beaufort was a changed woman after that day, but for the rest she was more herself than ever. The plight of refugee children is a thing which, when encountered face to face, will melt a far harder heart than Mrs. Beaufort's. She had not cared before simply because she had not seen. Now that she had seen, she cared very much -- in fact, in her own mind at least, she cared much more than anyone else did, and the only reason all the refugees were not fed and housed was that others did not feel their pain as she did.

This began a new set of trials, but it was an ending as well as a beginning, and the old, daily battles with Mrs. Creeley became less frequent and not so bitter. This was all the more important because of the events which soon followed. We needed each other then, all of us, and bound ourselves together, in spite of past differences, to face the present burdens of sorrow and fear.

First came the fall of France, and Hitler's triumphant entry into Paris. That was bad. I pictured the streets thronged with Nazis, the dreamy lamplight of evening spoiled by swastikas and the night music broken by guttural German shouts and whispers. The rhythm of marching feet filled the streets while a Frenchwoman watched for her sons and they did not come.

The fall of France brought Tristan back to England, but we saw little of him, for he was still flying missions. It was not the triumphant return to British soil that he had wished for, and his letters to Violet grew less cheerful as the time went on. I had seen him as a sort of gallant knight when he left for France, but on the first brief visit he paid us on his return, when he got away from the base on a short leave, I saw him changed. His face was harder, its lines cut deeper. I heard him say to Violet, "We all went in for glory, but all there is in war is death, and the only death with any glory in it is a quiet death at home after a long and peaceful life."

Perry also came to see us less often during that time, and his visits were shorter. He was often distracted when he did come, and Violet said he was very busy in a new position.

"He works with a special committee that works to find housing for the refugees," she said, with a look at Mrs. Beaufort, who brightened visibly at this introduction of her new favourite topic. "They have been busier than ever lately with all the French coming over."

Perry was instantly restored to favour in Mrs. Beaufort's eyes, and she forgot that she had ever criticised him. I could not forget what had been hinted at so easily, but I liked Perry still (indeed, it was impossible not to) and could not help but smile when I walked into the sitting room on several different occasions to find him asleep in the armchair with the newspaper spread across his lap or falling onto the floor.

I received one indignant letter from Gloria on the subject of the fall of France. Then came a surprisingly long break in our correspondence, and I heard nothing for several months after I had posted my reply. This came as quite a surprise to me, considering how regular (allowing for the unreliable nature of the post) she had been in her replies until then.

But soon I ceased to consider the post, or worry over things of that kind, for there came the blackest night in all our lives, the first of many spent in fear, huddled in the corner of the cellar. It was the night the Germans first bombed the city of London.

I shall not waste time making useless comparisons with other horrors, trying to create analogies which would only be flat and empty. It was like nothing I can find to compare it to. The thing we had feared the most since the war began had taken place, and the only thing for us to do was to grit our teeth and accept it with dogged patience.

We had all been trained from the beginning. Everyone had their bomb shelter in the garden, or, like us, a corner of the cellar reserved for such purposes. We kept stocks of food there, and we each had a little bag with some necessities, together with some old patchwork quilts, worked in bright blues and cheery yellows, and pillows, making the whole thing look rather more like a cosy retreat than a place to run to in fear.

We had heard the sirens before, false alarms or tests which came to nothing. Always, after the first sickening pangs of fear had assaulted my stomach and we had all hurried to the cellar the sirens would cease and the world would come right again. I had almost stopped feeling the knot grow in my insides at the sound.

But that night it did not stop. It went on, filling the night with an eerie, tuneless music, weird and relentless, which was soon joined by other sounds -- deafening, explosive sounds. Mr. and Mrs. Beaufort were huddled together among the blankets, and I could not see their faces. Mrs. Creeley crouched with her fingers in her ears, her teeth bared and eyes closed. Violet sat a little apart, very pale and very still, staring wide-eyed at nothing.

I found myself thinking of Perry. He had been with us earlier that day. Had he gone home to Ashford, or had he stayed in town? I prayed fervently that he was safe in the country.

In the odd way which sometimes happens in the middle of a crisis, I found myself noticing little, inconsequential things. The pattern of the quilt I held about me, the whiteness of my knuckles, together with the little red lines criss-crossed over them, the line of Violet's profile, which was all that I could see of her in the darkness, and the paradox presented by the mixed strength and fragility of that line -- all those things showed themselves to me in vivid detail, through my fear and the cacophony around me. So it went on for a while, and the strange thoughts kept at least a small corner of my mind free of fear, until at last all thought and feeling, including fear, collapsed, leaving only a wild desire for the noise to stop. I curled up into a compact little ball and covered my head with my arms.

I woke up there in the silence of morning, a silence which had never seemed so lovely, or so ominous. Was it the fresh silence of early morning, or was it the silence of death, of defeat? I could not remember hearing the bombs and sirens stop. None of us had moved in the night. We all lay in a heap of blankets. I was the first to wake, but the rest soon followed, rising out of the pile of quilts like strange wraiths with wild hair and dark-shadowed eyes, strange creases in their cheeks and strange groanings in their voices.

A few moments were spent by all in staring at the flight of steps leading upstairs, both wishing and fearing to ascend and investigate any damage. Violet was the first to get to her feet, and she stood for a time looking down at the rest of us. She said nothing, but I knew what she was asking with that silent look. Her expression said plainly, "Is there anyone here brave enough to climb those stairs with me?"

I rose to my feet and joined her.

We blundered up the stairs together, emerging at the top to find the house still standing. That important discovery made, and our minds more at rest about things in general because of it, we ventured out the front door and into the street, not caring that our clothes and hair were rumpled from an uneasy night spent buried in a heap of blankets.

We were not the only ones in such a state, however, and there were many others gathered on the street, blankets wrapped around their shoulders, blinking bleary eyes through forelocks of disheveled hair. For once nobody seemed to care about their appearance, and we shook hands cheerfully with our neighbours as everybody congratulated everybody else on surviving the night. Our immediate neighbourhood was undamaged, but smoke and dust rose in the distance, and their smells were everywhere.

Perry came in as we were sitting down to breakfast in a weak attempt to return to business as usual. He had intended to return to Ashford the night before, though he had a flat in London and often stayed there, but had been deterred by a friend's offer of dinner. They had sat up together until the bombing began, when they had taken refuge in one of the public shelters.

"I have come to try to persuade you to come out to Ashford with me today," he said to Mrs. Creeley, his usually merry face quite serious. "It is more dangerous than ever for you to stay here now, and completely unnecessary, when we could all fit together comfortably at home."

Mrs. Creeley pursed her lips, smiled, then frowned, and I gave up hope that she would accept the invitation.

"I have no doubt you mean it well, Perry," she said, quite gently for her, "but I won't do it -- not until the house falls down around my ears." Mrs. Beaufort groaned audibly. "I told Tristan once already, and I did think that you at least would understand and not push me. Ever since poor Adam died I've been determined to live on my own and accept charity from no one as long as I am able. Surely you wouldn't ask me to give up my independence when you know how much it means to me."

By the end of this short speech her voice had taken on an almost pleading tone. I could not have refused her. I doubt even Mrs. Beaufort could have done that, and Perry was a closer sympathiser of hers than any of us. He could not approve her decisions, but neither could he take away her dignity. Mrs. Beaufort looked eager, as if she hoped that an offer would be made to the rest of us, leaving Mrs. Creeley alone in London to enjoy her independence alone. Perry looked at Violet, raising one eyebrow in a questioning way, but Violet only shook her head, as I had expected. I thought it strange that he looked to me next, and not to the Beauforts, but he did, and I shook my head as well, though I heard Mrs. Beaufort heave a heavy sigh as I did so. If Violet had chosen to stay with the old lady through everything, I would not desert her.

That decided the matter, and no more was said for the present about leaving town. Perry stayed to lunch with us, and our cheerfulness returned in the light of day with the ease his presence brought. We had just finished eating and were sitting together around the table, laughing over some news Perry brought from Ashford, when we heard a knock on the front door.

I happened to be nearest to the hall, and I jumped up in the middle of a laugh to open the door. Then I stood staring. It was Gloria.

13

My thoughts were muddled. I was glad to see her, of course, more than glad. I had wished for her often, and had missed her stimulating influence. Yet, at the same time, why had she come? Her presence now explained the break in our correspondence which had troubled me, yet again, why re-cross an ocean, returning from safety to danger? My mind returned to the mayhem of the night before. That was what Gloria had returned to, though she could not have known that when she began her journey. I shuddered.

"You look like you just saw a moose fly by with blue bows round its antlers." She was laughing. "Aren't you glad to see me, Anna?"

Her words brought me back to a somewhat clearer idea of where I was and what I was doing. I hugged her.

"Of course I'm glad," I said, "just so surprised I didn't know what to do or say at first. Come in, and tell me what made you decide to come back."

She stepped into the hall.

"Well," she said, "you know how frustrated I was with the old ladies back home, trying to get something done for the cause and all they could think of was a knitting group, right? You can do so much more over here, you're so much closer to things. I just couldn't take it any longer and came myself. I wasn't expecting to arrive just before a bombing raid, but they kept us safe once we got off the boat and I'm here now."

"Gloria," I said, hesitantly, "I hem shirts and dig potatoes."

"I know, but there must be so many more opportunities, not just that, so much more everyone could be doing. I could take nurse's training here."

I tried not be hurt by the implication that I should be doing more. I knew there were young women training to become nurses in the city's hospitals, which were already filling with our wounded soldiers, and I knew, in a vague sort of way, that many were my age and some even younger, but the possibility that I might become one had never entered my head. They seemed a breed apart, a bit like the soldiers themselves, born heroes who lived for that purpose. It was a ridiculous thought when I finally brought it out of the depths of my unconscious and examined it, like saying that butterflies were born as butterflies and never started out as ugly little caterpillars. But soldiers and nurses were much tougher things than butterflies, and much uglier than caterpillars, perhaps because of the dreadful, bloody cocoon they were forced to squeeze their way out of. It was a poor analogy, but I couldn't get it out of my head. I was thinking nonsense again.

I shook my head to clear it of strange wandering thoughts, and Gloria looked a little offended, as if I was shaking my head at her idea of nurse's training. I suppose that is how it looked. She could not have been expected to read my mind. I almost said something, but she spoke first.

"I expect I will find somewhere to stay soon, near the hospitals if I decide to do the nurse's training, but would it be too much to ask to stay here until then?"

"No, you must stay with us, of course, and not think of leaving at all. I'm sure the others will feel the same way." All, except perhaps Mrs. Creeley.

I led the way into the sitting room. I was glad that Perry was still there. I felt that he would support me and help me to smooth over an awkward situation, as he had done often enough on other occasions.

It was not to be so, however, for when we entered the sitting room I saw to my disappointment that Perry had fallen asleep in his chair, while everyone else sat staring at us, very much awake. I felt an irrational stab of frustration and for one moment wanted to cross the room to shake Perry out of his sleep and reproach him for failing me.

I shook myself instead. It was not right to expect anyone to take care of this for me. My sense of something vaguely ridiculous in my reaction to the situation helped me to say, "You all remember Gloria, don't you? She's come back to London to help, and I've offered her a home here with us."

Mr. and Mrs. Beaufort both smiled and said how nice it was to see her again, but they looked confused. Violet nodded without a word. Mrs. Creeley looked slightly thunderous. I said nothing for a few minutes, searching for the right words, but I was saved the trouble of a longer explanation, for Gloria stepped forward and began to speak for herself, and I relapsed into grateful silence. It was better, after all, that they should hear an account from her own lips.

She made the explanation plain and concise, but it was delivered with all the ease and charm of her nature at its best and could not fail to win over her audience. It was her great gift – to persuade with a smile and win over even tough old ladies to her way of thinking. Mrs. Creeley was one of the toughest old ladies going, yet though she refused to return Gloria's smile or express anything like joy at the prospect of another long-term guest in her house, she did not reject the idea outright and even told Violet and me to prepare the sofa in our room for another sleeper.

Perry had roused himself by then. Just in time, I thought rather unjustly, to miss all the discomfort. He remembered Gloria from our meeting in the park before her departure, and made her welcome with better grace than any of the rest of us had managed. The mood of the room lightened by degrees, and the pleasantness returned.

Gloria had left her suitcase in the hall. Violet and I went together to take it upstairs and prepare the sofa for her as soon as the question was decided. Gloria remained behind with our elders, drawn into a conversation with Mrs. Beaufort concerning last night's bombing.

"Why did she come?"

"What?" Violet had asked the question as we were bumping up the stairs with Gloria's suitcase. In truth I had heard her well enough. My "what?" was brought on, not by lack of clarity but by something in her tone which bordered on the uncharitable.

She looked a little embarrassed, and I gathered that she had not meant to speak her thought aloud.

"It's only that there are already so many refugees looking for somewhere to sleep, and more are coming every day," she said apologetically. "I say nothing against her motives. I'm sure she meant it well, but the house might be bombed tomorrow, and then what would any of us do? Tristan writes about the American pilots he works with very often, and I don't mean to say anything against what they do to help us, but there are bases and quarters provided for those men. It's different from this somehow. It sounds horrible to say it but there is a kind of help that burdens those it came to help more than it aids them."

She broke off as if unable to complete her thought, and waved her free arm.

"I said more than I intended. I'm sorry, Anna. It's so easy to become a little bitter these days."

She was blushing with frustration at herself. It was the most emotional I had ever seen her. My mind went back to something she had said.

"What if the house is bombed tomorrow?" I wanted to direct the conversation away from Gloria, but I admit my choice of subject was rather grim.

"If we are not killed, then we will all go to Ashford – your friend Gloria too if she wishes. Perry's offers are always genuine."

She said the first half of this speech very matter-of-factly, the second with a smile of renewed tranquility.

I didn't mean to say it, but we had reached the bedroom and were all alone, and it seemed to be a day for blurting things out, if there are ever days allotted for that sort of thing.

"Why doesn't Perry fight with the others?"

Melanie Rose

14

My question sounded so dreadfully bare to my own ears. No introduction of topic. No mellowing of subject. I might as well have asked, "Is Perry a coward?" straight out. It came to the same thing.

But Violet was looking at me with a smile on her lips.

"Didn't you know?" she asked.

"Know what?"

"Perry has Narcolepsy."

I stared at her. I had heard the word before, but I had no more idea of its meaning than I had of the domestic habits of dung beetles.

"There aren't many people who know what it is," said Violet. To my surprise, she was laughing.

"I'm sorry Anna," she went on "but I can imagine what you must have been thinking. Put simply, Narcoleptics fall asleep at uncertain times. It sounds slight enough, but it's completely uncontrollable, and you could imagine how that would be in the middle of a war zone. It's also why Perry doesn't drive."

I checked to make sure the door was shut, then threw back my head and laughed with her. I was filled with such relief, and it seemed ridiculously funny as well that this thing which had troubled me for so long had an answer which I never would have guessed but which solved the riddle so perfectly. I had imagined so many possible scenarios, but never this one, and never one which tied up all loose ends and uncertainties as this did. I thought of my first meeting with Perry, how he had fallen asleep and dropped his newspaper on the floor and his dictionary on my toe, and there had been a string of instances since then – finding out that he did not drive, walking into a room and finding him asleep, or just today when Gloria and I had come into the room and he had been dozing in his chair.

"He took it very hard at first," said Violet, becoming serious again once our first impulse of laughter had worn off. "You can imagine how it must have been, when Tristan was going, as well as other friends he'd grown up with in the country. He does what work he can in London, and goes back and forth between Ashford and town several times a month. He's found homes for a lot of the refugees, and that's his main work now, but sometimes I think he's still disappointed in himself, that he couldn't go to the front. He's looked so much older these last few years, since it first seemed like a war might be unavoidable, and I worry about him sometimes. He's only twenty-six you know."

I thought of that first day in the train, when he had reminded me of my uncle Nicholas, but I only said, "Well it's a good thing for everyone else that he couldn't go. What would Mrs. Creeley do without him, or the family at Ashford? He makes himself indispensable, even just for keeping all of us here from ripping each other's hair out."

We both went downstairs again with tempers much improved by our mutual bluntness. I felt well-disposed towards everybody. Violet was becoming a good friend and I thought Perry bore his trial marvellously well. The Beauforts meant to be kind and were harmless and amusing enough, while even Mrs. Creeley probably meant well under her gruffness. As for Gloria, she had never looked so lovely to me as when Violet and I came down the stairs and into the sitting room and I saw her there (the centre of that room as of every other) enthralling her audience with an account of her voyage.

With characteristic energy Gloria went out the next day to look into the idea of nurse's training. She came back tired but triumphant with the announcement that she was to start in three days, and we all congratulated her on the success of her enterprise, though out of the corner of my eye I saw that Violet eyed her with something akin to dislike. When Gloria was in highest spirits, Violet was lowest, and it seemed to me as if Gloria's brightness scorched the soul of the younger, quieter girl – strange that the thing which had so drawn me to one should repel the other. Violet always maintained a careful guard over her expressions, and rarely let anything slip. If I had not been her daily companion for many months by that time I would never have seen the swiftly hidden changes of expression which passed from time to time over her countenance.

The bombings continued, but the shivers that had gone down my spine at the first eerie sound of the sirens never grew less, even when I heard them every night for days at a time. Mrs. Creeley took to stuffing large wads of cotton in her ears every evening, before the wailing of the sirens even began. She claimed that it helped to muffle the noise and calm her nerves, but since she was just as quick to hear a whisper from any of us with it as she was without it, I found myself doubting whether it really did any good at all. Mrs. Beaufort's nightly panic began in a very systematic way a little before dinner, and was generally raised to its highest pitch just before the bombing began, after which she would subside, whimpering, in a pile of blankets. As Gloria whispered to me at dinner one night, "She's the first person I've met with the ability to turn hyperventilation into an exact science."

Mr. Beaufort would watch his wife in a helpless sort of way, not daring to approach her until she collapsed, then settle into a sitting position beside her and pat her head, looking straight ahead of him with wide, blank, staring eyes.

I had to esteem Gloria more than ever for her behaviour during the bombing raids. The noise did not seem to trouble her, and she was a comfort to everyone from the beginning. Even Violet gave her an admiring glance on the first night, when she passed out bread and cheese to the rest of us with smiling nonchalance as the sirens shrieked and the bombs exploded in the distance.

To all of us looking on it seemed that the nurse's training was progressing well and according to plan. Gloria came home each night in great spirits, only with a little impatience to be done with the training and begin the great work of helping to save lives.

Tristan came home for a week's leave that autumn, and it was then that Violet's tolerance of Gloria was tested most severely. Anyone can imagine what the outcome might possibly be, putting a handsome young man straight from war and mayhem into a house inhabited by a sister, a great-aunt, and four guests, one of whom is a beautiful, self-possessed young woman. Gloria was prepared to be admired, and Tristan was equally prepared to admire her, and the new lines I had observed in his face smoothed out and his easy charm returned. The piano in the sitting room, which had grown accustomed to dust and disuse, was brought out from its corner and played every evening for the week that Tristan was home. We all loved to hear her play. For me it brought back memories of our earlier time together, travelling through France when the war was merely a hazy threat.

It was on one of those evenings, as I was sitting in a corner enjoying the picture made by Gloria's seated figure at the piano and the tall form of Tristan leaning against it looking down at her, that I happened to glance at Violet, who sat near me, on the other side of Perry, who had fallen asleep and thus did not screen her from my sight. The light was dim. The only illumination came from the small lamp on the piano, and it showed little with clarity except the keys of the instrument and the faces bent over it, but one ray of reflected light came from the mirror over the fireplace and lit upon Violet's face. It was the first time since Gloria's arrival that I had seen her face unguarded. Her eyes were intent on Gloria's face, and there was jealousy in them, jealousy marked with a kind of contempt, but also, I noted with surprise, a touch of something like pity. She blinked, as if she was trying to clear dust from her eyes, and her gaze moved to her brother as he stood looking down at the performer with her halo of brilliant hair and her smiling features. The eyes softened while they watched his profile against the lamplight, softened into a tender sadness that made her face seem suddenly lovely to me. Perhaps it is strange that I had never noticed that subtle beauty before, but I can only say in my defence that it was a beauty not suited to crowds and bright lights. Compared with Gloria's brilliance, Violet was like a tiny alpine flower beside some exotic bloom of the tropics, a hibiscus or a bird-of-paradise. It can be easily hidden, but once truly seen it is never forgotten.

  I must have stared too intently. Before I realised it the music was over and Violet had turned to see me watching her. She bent her head quickly to hide a faint blush, and when she raised her eyes the guarded look had returned.

  Gloria was saying something to Tristan. I saw her look up at him and smile, then look grave as she said, loud enough for the rest of us to hear, "They say tomorrow will be the real test. They're putting us in the hospital with real patients. Some girls can't take it, I hear, and have to be sent home because they can't stand the sight of blood." There was a cheerful disdain in her voice, not malicious, but amused -- the disdain of someone with a good head for heights standing at the edge of a cliff and looking back at the people who have kept their distance.

Mr. Beaufort beamed at her from the depths of his armchair. "We all know that will never be you, my girl. You've got too much gumption for that."

Tristan smiled down at her and said something I couldn't quite hear. She looked up at him and laughed.

"No," she said, "I don't think I'd be afraid of that either."

15

Tristan was leaving the next day, and as Gloria had to be at the hospital in the morning he offered to accompany her and go on his own way from there. So we bid them both good-bye at once at the front door. I was glad to see that Violet and Tristan had been able to spend some time by themselves in the garden earlier, and Violet was looking better for it, even to the point of wishing Gloria good luck for her first day at the hospital. She said her good-byes to her brother without shedding tears, though when she turned away I could see them standing in her eyes.

We went out for groceries later that day, and as we passed St. Paul's Cathedral I remembered the time when Gloria and I had climbed to the very top and looked out over London. I asked Violet if she had ever made the climb.

"Yes." She said it shyly, as if she were confessing something very close to her heart. "I used to go often, before you came. I came here the first time with Tristan, years ago. Then later, when Grandmother would send me out for groceries alone I would come here first and climb to the top and look out over the city and think about things. It felt wonderful, like you were so far away from everything that no trouble could reach you."

It was just how I had felt, and after hesitating a moment I said, "Would you like to go up now?"

We climbed the long stair together, at first in company with a few others, but soon alone as those climbing with us grew tired or dizzy and stopped. At last we stood at the very top, surrounded by the golden railing, and we looked out over the city. I knew it better now. I could pick out bits of the scene with my eyes and knew their names and how to reach them on foot without getting lost.

We stood there for a long time in complete silence. It was only when all the church clocks of the city began to strike twelve that we turned and left the pinnacle to return to the world beneath.

After we had collected all the groceries, I suggested, my curiosity having been piqued, that we should take a detour to walk by the hospital where Gloria was to be working. Violet agreed, and we turned about a little in our walk so that it took us by St. Bartholomew's, near Smithfield.

The hospital was a noble-looking building, large and solid. We walked around it, looking up at it and thinking of the poor patients inside, and then were about to turn for home when I caught a flash of red hair in the outdoor seating area of a nearby pub.

Red hair, even of that brilliance, is not an improbable thing to see on the street in London, but it always made me think of Gloria, so I turned and looked more closely at the figure.

It was Gloria. She was sitting by herself at one of the pub tables with a pint of beer in front of her, and she was crying. I stood amazed. Not only had I never seen her cry before, but I had never known her to drink anything stronger than lemonade and the mug was nearly empty. I exchanged concerned glances with Violet, who would never have wished ill on Gloria no matter how much she disliked her, and we ran across the street to the pub.

Gloria did not appear to see us until we were standing just beside the table looking down at her. When she did see us she said nothing at first, only cried harder.

I sat down beside her and put my arm around her while Violet stood by awkwardly.

"Tell me what happened," I said. I could do nothing to help her while I had no idea what the problem was.

"I...am...so embarrassed..." she finally managed to sob out "after last night. But it wasn't the blood. The blood was terrible, of course, but it wasn't what made me faint. It was his leg. It was just...gone... and there was bone, just sticking out, and I felt dizzy and then he grabbed my arm and told me he needed something for the pain, and then he smiled like he was making some horrible kind of joke and told me that a kiss from me would make his leg feel like nothing and...and then I fainted."

She coughed, took another drink, and then said, laughing a little, "Was it funny? Should I have been laughing? Why couldn't I laugh then? It might have made him feel better. But I'm laughing now. Have you come to take me back? They won't take me back, you know? They can't have nurses fainting all the time. It...won't...do." She emphasised the last three words by banging her mug on the table.

I felt helpless. My grandmother thought all alcohol was of the devil, thus I had never had much experience with drunk people before and I had no idea what to do for her. On top of that, when I looked around I could see nothing of Violet. Why had she left me here like this? I tightened my hold around Gloria's shoulders and patted her hand with my free one.

"It's going to be all right," I told her, hardly knowing what I said. "Everyone will understand."

"But what about Tristan?" she sobbed, taking another drink, though I had tried to move her mug some distance away on the table. "He told me last night that I was the pluckiest girl he'd ever met. But it's not true, and he'll find out eventually. Then what will he think of me?"

She swayed in her seat and I did my best to support her with my arm while I wracked my brains for something comforting to say in reply. After several minutes of this mental anguish I felt a tap on my shoulder and turned to see Violet standing there.

"There's a cab waiting," she whispered. "We can use what is left of the grocery money to pay for it. Even Grandmother will understand when it's something like this."

Between the two of us we tried to support Gloria to the cab, but she really was very far gone and gave us no assistance. I wondered how much she'd had before we arrived. However, before we had gone very far I heard a voice at my elbow say, "Come to collect your friend at last, have you? Move aside and let me give her my arm. Things are bad indeed when a pretty lass drinks alone and has to be picked up by her friends before the sun's even begun to set."

He was an older man, in his sixties or seventies, but tall and strong, and once he had motioned Violet and myself out of the way he picked Gloria up in his arms as if she was a baby and carried her to the waiting cab. I stopped just long enough to pay the pub keeper before I hurried after them.

We got her into the house easily enough, and up the stairs to our bedroom, where she immediately went to sleep. Without too much explanation, but enough to stop the endless flow of questions, we got Mr. and Mrs. Beaufort and Mrs. Creeley to understand a little about the nature of the case. Then Mrs. Creeley took over, and it was a marvel indeed to see her work.

"My husband was a good man," she said, "but he did like his drink now and then, and he did take too much once in a while. We can make her more comfortable now, but she'll have a little bit of a headache when she wakes up."

At first we intended to leave her in our room to rest, but it was getting later, and if the bombing began none of us wanted to carry her downstairs again with the sirens going off and mayhem all around us. So we carried her down then and there and laid her on a pile of blankets in the corner of the cellar which we had begun to refer to with daring fondness as "The Drop Zone".

Violet and I had dreaded questions about Gloria's state and her expulsion from the hospital, but our fears were unfounded. The bombings did continue that night, and in the morning we had things to think about which put the events of that day entirely in the background.

Melanie Rose

16

I woke up after an even more restless night than usual to find Mrs. Beaufort shaking me. The air of the cellar was close and oppressive. At first I thought it must still be night, for the shaft of light which usually came through from under the door at the top of the stairs was gone, and all was dark and still. But the stillness did not have the feel of night, and one glance at the clock near my blanket nest told me that it was nearly six in the morning.

Gloria was fast asleep beside me, and I thought it would take some work to wake her – more work than I was ready to put in just then, anyway.

"What's happened?" I asked Mrs. Beaufort, though the look on her face told me plainly that she could hardly know more about it than I did.

"I don't know," she whimpered. "Beaufort thinks something may have collapsed at the top of the stairs." I got up and walked to the foot of the stairway. Her voice followed me. "What do you think, Anna?"

When had I become chaperone? I looked curiously up the stairs. The door itself looked solid enough at the top, only there was no light coming from underneath it.

Mrs. Beaufort quavered, "What if the doorway is blocked?"

Now was not a good time for her to panic. I heard Mr. Beaufort whisper, "Hush, my love. At the worst we'll just have to wait here until someone comes to dig us out." I wished he would keep his words of comfort to himself. I started climbing.

"Be careful dear." They had followed me as far as the foot of the stairs. I was not feeling like anybody's dear.

I reached the door. I could hear more motion from below, as Violet and Mrs. Creeley awoke. I hesitated. Then the ridiculous side of the situation occurred to me. Why did I hesitate? Wouldn't it be better just to know the worst? Our boys went into battle face to face with death in the form of armed German soldiers, and I was afraid to open a door. I turned the handle.

The door opened easily. I turned triumphantly to call back, "The door is open." Then the sight on the other side of the door struck me like a hard slap in the face with a wet towel, knocking the breath out of me.

My first thought was that this place was no longer Mrs. Creeley's house. It was a pile of debris which slightly resembled a place where we had all lived long ago, but it was not that place. My second thought was that we had been lucky, so lucky.

The house had not been hit directly, as it turned out, but had been shaken like a tree in a high wind by a nearby explosion. A beam had fallen from the ceiling, crashing down on the lintel of the cellar door. I thanked God that Mrs. Creeley's house had been well-built. The lintel was a great piece of oak, weathered with age but still strong, and though it sagged and splintered under the weight of the beam, it still held, if barely. The rest of the house was a mess, and the absence of light was explained by the tumble of plaster and furnishings obscuring the spaces where there had once been windows, but I thought I saw an opening through which we might pass to the outside world.

I hurried back down the cellar stairs, calling to the others.

"It could only be a matter of time before all the rest comes crashing down on our heads," I said. "We need to get out while we can."

Ignoring Mrs. Beaufort's panic, which had been growing since she woke up and was now almost at full pitch, I joined Violet and Mrs. Creeley, who were proving themselves more practical by each taking a side of Gloria and shaking her into wakefulness.

"What is it?" Her voice was drowsy, and she pressed a hand to her forehead, wincing.

It was Mrs. Creeley who answered her.

"Anna's gone up and found the house half gone," she said, with a dry calm in her voice. A stranger would never have thought that the house she had lived in for most of her life had just been destroyed. "We need to get out before it falls down on top of us."

While Mrs. Creeley was giving this brief explanation, the rest of us had been hurriedly bundling up the most important things from The Drop Zone to take out with us in case what remained of the house did indeed collapse and leave us with no hope of retrieving anything.

Gloria scrambled to her feet and joined us, groaning a little and holding her head as she rose, but alluding in no other way to the dreadful headache we all knew she was having.

In just a few more minutes we all stood at the top of the steps with our bundles, looking about for the clearest path through the rubble. There was some stooping involved, and stepping over and sliding between what was left of the kitchen counter and the fallen, smashed hulk of what had once been the china cabinet, but with no greater obstacles than these we did at last reach the open air of the street, sort of.

Debris was everywhere. A house nearby had suffered a direct hit, and there seemed to be nothing of it left except for a little pile of splinters, like the shavings left over from a giant's whittling. On the street, lying amid the rubble, bits of people's lives were scattered, like rose petals strewn over new-made graves. I saw a pocket comb, a bit of blue ribbon, a green umbrella, a broken-framed photograph of a girl with a pony, a letter ending "love, Jim". The tears came to my eyes, but did not fall. I could feel them hovering on the brink, but there were more important things to think of than tears just then, and I swallowed them as I joined the others in laying down our bundles in a pile and beginning the search for other survivors.

Most of the houses were in the same condition as Mrs. Creeley's and had not been hit directly, only shaken and smashed sideways, like the houses in a gingerbread village which the hungry dog has knocked over with his wagging tail on his way to devour the one he desires.

With a sort of fevered energy we turned our attention to the houses which had received direct hits, calling out from time to time as we pulled away rubbish looking for a cellar entrance or an area which had somehow escaped demolition. It was not long before more professional rescuers arrived in the form of a group of officers. Perry accompanied them in his official capacity of civil servant, though his air of cool authority broke down for a moment or two into a relieved grin when he saw us alive and unhurt.

The officers spread out and searched the wreckage much more systematically than we had done, while we stood back to make way for them. For a long time we stood there, watching but not seeing. The first spasmodic energy of our escape from the musty cellar had dissipated and now I felt empty. Only my skin and bones stood there in the street. My soul was elsewhere, detached, observing the scene but not a part of it.

It was Perry's voice which brought soul back to body, inquiring if we were all whole and well. He was standing by my shoulder, and Violet was on his other side. Together we stood like a house of cards, leaning against each other in our fragility, only thus making a standing structure. I felt safer with them both there. My courage of the morning had ebbed and I was afraid again, afraid with a childish fear that was an echo of what I had felt when, at the age of six, I had asked a man in a white coat where my mother was and had known from his silent look at my grandmother that my parents were dead.

Perry was speaking again, telling us to go to his London flat and wait for him there. He would join us later when his work was done for the day. We could get cleaned up and rested there and the next day he would go with us to Ashford.

"Parts of the house are still standing," said Mrs. Creeley. "I don't want to just walk away while there's still a chance that we might be able to salvage something." Her words were steady and calm, with a return of their usual biting quality, but I could see that she was tottering a little on her legs, and her hands were shaky as she patted her hair into a slightly less wild mess.

"I'll make a point of going in with a few officers to see if we can retrieve anything before we leave the area," he said calmly "Don't worry. Just go with the rest and I'll be there this evening with whatever we find."

"Imagine a bunch of men going through an old woman's odds and ends. It's hardly decent. You'd probably throw away the best of it and keep things I don't care two straws about."

I groaned inwardly. She was just being difficult for the sake of being difficult, like she always did on her peevish days, but it could keep us there for the rest of the day sorting through bits of partially demolished lampshades.

But Perry was used to her, and used to dealing with her foibles. Compromise was sometimes necessary, as was firmness, and this time he employed both.

"I will keep one or two of the girls here to help me decide, if that will give you ease," he said, "but you are going to my flat this minute with the others to rest yourself."

"Very well, you may have Violet and Anna if they can be useful," she said with the air of someone conferring a great favour by offering the loan of a cart horse. "Gloria would be no help. She doesn't know my things, and besides" with a return of the old veiled amusement I remembered from my first meeting with her, "she had a hard night last night."

So they left us with Perry in the midst of the rubble, and in spite of my weariness and insecurity I thought I would rather remain there with those two than go with the others to argue about who would bathe first and then fall asleep in a corner. The very nature of my mind's weariness made physical exertion a necessity. I had to keep moving, working, or my brain would crumble in on itself.

That day was the longest I had ever experienced, but when it was over Violet and Perry and I had a quiet walk through the city to Perry's flat, stopping for ice cream on the way in spite of the chilly twilight of early spring.

London seemed almost spectral to me as we walked through it. Even the crowded clubs, full of the indomitable population, seemed more like echoes of yesterday than real, living, vibrant sounds of today. How could such things exist in reality when only yards away smoke rose from the ruins of people's homes and lost remnants of their lives smouldered into ashes in the dusk?

Still, in some parts of the city you could almost forget the war -- almost, but not quite. We walked slowly beside the river to London Bridge and crossed over, talking of small things -- the water, the buildings, the passers-by, but never the war -- and I thought of crossing the Ponte Vecchio in Florence. Just over a year gone, yet it felt so much longer ago and farther away, like an early childhood memory painted in pale, fading colours.

We lingered for some time in the middle of the bridge, watching the river and the last scraps of sunset fading on the horizon before we continued on our way. It was a fine night, but in spite of that I shivered. We had all come to welcome stormy nights because they generally meant a break in the stream of air-raids.

The sirens were beginning as we turned into Perry's street.

Melanie Rose

17

The station master at Wells knew Perry from his frequent trips to and from London.

"More homeless come to join the Bertram household," he joked, looking down over his large, rubicund nose at us with our baggage. His tone was obviously meant to be genial but I found it somewhat unpleasant and his jaws were constantly in motion with the regularity of a mechanical nutcracker, as if he chewed his thoughts into paste before spitting them at people.

Perry answered him curtly. "Not homeless, Chester. Friends and relatives coming to stay for a while."

Chester stared at us in silence for a moment, though the perambulation of his jaws continued. Then he muttered something inaudible and waved us on.

"Don't mind Chester," said Perry as we walked down the platform. "He's not a bad chap, but he's a Sedgewick. That won't mean anything to you now, of course, but it will soon if you spend much time in Wells. Almost without exception the Sedgewick men are pessimistic and the women are melancholy."

Mr. Bertram was waiting in the rain with the family automobile. He was fairly tall, though not so tall as his son, a robust man with salt-and-pepper hair, kind eyes, and mild manners. At first glance I thought there was not much resemblance between him and Perry, but then he looked at me and smiled and I thought that any likeness between them had its root in that smile. It spread from the lips to the eyes and created nice crinkles in their corners.

Mr. Bertram greeted his son, as well as Violet and Mrs. Creeley, with warmth and familial affection, then turned to the rest of us.

"You are all very welcome," he said kindly, taking each of our hands in turn. "My son has told me so much about you that you already seem like part of the family. I'm sure we will all get on very well together, and I hope you will be comfortable at Ashford."

I was last in line, and as he came up to me and took my hand his smile, if possible, seemed to grow kinder, and he said, "You must be Anna. You are just how Perry described you."

I blushed a little at this extra attention, wondering at the same time what had been said about me, rather surprised that it was me and not Gloria who received this attention. Judging from Mr. Bertram's manner I tried to tell myself that the description must have been favourable, but then I recalled what Violet had often said about her uncle's passion for sick, crippled and deformed animals and gave up trying to decide.

Squished into the Bertram family automobile with our baggage we were like sardines in olive oil. Violet and Gloria and I, at the extreme rear of the vehicle, were the most tightly packed of all, practically sitting in each other's laps with baggage under, over and between us.

The beauty of the drive more than made up for the tightness of the circumstances, however, and I gradually became lost to the discomfort, as well as to any conversation going on within the car. Several times I had to be shaken back into reality by my companions to answer questions directed at me by Mr. Bertram, though in my defence the many noises -- rain on the roof of the car, voices, bumping of baggage as we went round the corners -- were nearly as much to blame as my abstraction of mind.

Yet even surrounded by the rain-washed beauty of the encircling landscape, it was the first glimpse of Ashford that I longed for most, though there was something like fear mingled with the longing. The house and garden had taken such possession of my imagination that the images entrenched there had nearly as much hold on me as reality. What if it were not quite the same as what I imagined? If it were not quite so wonderful? If you turned left rather than right from the back door to come to the well? If the wild rabbits didn't come onto the edge of the lawn and wriggle their noses quite as Violet had described them. Small things, yet together they made up the image of perfection I had woven about the thought of Ashford, and I worried that my own mind might perhaps betray me into disappointment.

It was early afternoon when we reached the tiny village of Nettlebridge, on the far side of which Ashford awaited our arrival, and the prevailing mood in the car was one of hunger. We had not lunched on the way, for Mr. Bertram had informed us that a substantial meal was planned to welcome us. The mood was intensified by the description our host gave us of the meal to come, adding with emphasis that his household (meaning his wife Lilly, his mother, and a girl from the village who came in to help sometimes in exchange for produce from the garden) did amazing things with food even on wartime rations.

"Sometimes Jerry helps them," he added "and then you end up with some unusual combinations of flavours -- sage in the pudding or cinnamon on the sausages for instance -- but it's all done with the best motives, and as often as not we're all astonished by how good it is."

I saw Mrs. Beaufort shudder. Violet and I smiled at each other across the baggage. She had told me of Jerry's bold ventures into the culinary arts before.

We drove slowly through the village, turned up a little hill on the other side, rounded a corner and there was Ashford.

It was the most homelike place I had ever seen. Mr. Bertram parked the car in a small shed some distance from the main house, and we walked up to it by a footpath through an orchard of twisted apple trees. They were still leafless, but I found that I was glad of that. I wanted to see spring unfold from its beginning in this place.

The house itself -- large but not ostentatiously so, like a manor that is not quite sure it deserves the name -- was covered in masses of ivy, with diamond-paned windows glinting through at intervals. I heard Mrs. Creeley say to Mr. Bertram, "You really need to put in new windows Edward. One gets behind those things and can hardly see out." But I knew exactly what the world would look like through their tiny panes, because Violet had told me. It would be slightly warped, softened, with the colours blending. It would be like looking into a different world, and even in its imperfection it would be perfect, because it was part of Ashford.

Mr. Bertram opened a door at the side of the house which led into the kitchen, and held it wide for us to enter. My first impression of the inside of the house was of warmth and scent. A large fire burned on a wide hearth, with a steaming pot hanging suspended over it from an ancient hook, though a modern gas stove stood nearby unused. An alluringly savoury smell came from the pot, and the fragrance of lavender reached me from several bunches which hung drying from the ceiling. The aroma of cinnamon tickled my nose, and I smiled to myself, wondering if it flavoured sausages or something more appealing. The kitchen was immense and somewhat dim. I saw electric lights, but they had not been turned on, though lit candles stood here and there on table and sideboard. I remembered hearing about how long Perry's grandmother had held out against electricity, only giving way when Tristan enlisted and the radio reports became a necessity to control the anxiety of the household.

A figure sat in a chair by the far side of the fire, stirring the contents of the pot and reminding me of a storybook illustration of a gnome that I remembered from my childhood. In the illustration he was sitting just like that (only on a rock in a field by a tiny campfire) cooking his dinner, with the firelight shining on his face and lighting up his melancholy dark eyes and little black pointed beard. His eyes looked as though they held secrets which he didn't know how to tell.

He jumped up when he saw us, and the sorrowful look was erased, giving place to a cheerful expression of welcome as he hurried forward to greet us and take our baggage.

"Mother and Grandmother weren't expecting you so soon and are upstairs with the children," he said, "but I knew you'd be early. Come in and take off your coats." He was taking each of us by the arm in turn in a friendly, familiar way and pushing us eagerly towards the fire, but when he got to Gloria he stopped. He seemed fascinated by her (as everybody was) but also strangely afraid, and he shrunk back a little as he asked her in an awed whisper, "Are you the princess?"

She said, "No" in a voice of mixed confusion and amusement, and they stood staring at each other for a moment, until he turned away with a hurried, "I'll tell them you're here" and scuttled out of the room.

Mr. Bertram put a hand on Gloria's shoulder.

"Don't mind Jerry," he said. "There was an accident, when he was a very small child, and he's never been the same. But he used to love hearing fairy tales, and he's dreamed of seeing a real princess ever since. Sometimes I think he sees his whole life in the context of a fairy tale now, that what he lost most in the accident was the ability to see any difference between fantasy and reality."

Gloria nodded and smiled, but there was no time for any of us to speak before we heard the sound of returning footsteps approaching the kitchen.

The procession was led by a large English Sheepdog, so shaggy that her mild brown eyes looked out from behind a thick curtain of hair, reminding me of pictures I had seen of wild mountain men from the old American west. Two small children peered out from behind the dog, her bulk almost enough to hide their small forms from notice, and I guessed that they must be the twin refugee children from Poland whose parents had gone missing, Cyryl and Haline. A little old lady with a gentle, smiling face followed behind them leaning on a twisted walking stick. Her hair floated about her head in an ethereal cloud, giving her the appearance of a benign old fairy godmother. I found myself thinking that in this setting, with these people, it was small wonder that Jerry had invented a fairy-tale world for himself.

Last of all came Lilly Bertram, drifting into the kitchen on the tail of the procession as if she had forgotten about us completely and just happened to arrive there at the perfect time by some happy accident. She smiled at Perry in delighted surprise and crossed the room with a gliding step to put her hands on his shoulders and kiss his cheek. As she passed me I caught the scent of her perfume. It was like the memory of violets buried under damp fallen leaves, sweet yet vaguely fermented. She wore her dark hair down and it fell in thick waves to her waist, in striking contrast to her pale face and the delicate green dress she wore. I knew she was at least forty-five, but her air was one of youth. Age remembers, but she seemed to move within a circle of forgotten things, young forever.

With his usual tact Perry succeeded in turning his mother's attention to the rest of us.

"Welcome," she said. Her voice was soft, with a hint of music to it, and I remembered Violet telling me that she was part Welsh. "I hope your journey was pleasant."

Mrs. Creeley was first to answer.

"Well, if you took away the rain, and that awful cramped ride in your husband's car (which, by the by, appears to be falling to pieces) not to mention the fact that we're all fainting from hunger, it would have been passable."

But she was smiling.

Melanie Rose

18

Those first few days at Ashford were filled with childish adventure for me. Everything was fresh and new, touched with mystery, and for five days I woke up each morning forgetful of the war and its ugliness, thinking only of the day just dawned and the loveliness around me.

With Violet and Perry as guides and companions I rambled about the garden, the village, the fields and the nearby Harridge Woods, not caring for cold or wet, lost to everything but the thrill of discovery. I saw Violet as she must have been growing up there, as a happy little girl, gentle and smiling and ready to follow brother or cousin wherever they led with the boldness of complete trust. I saw Perry, free from professional responsibility, drop the sense of age which he wore in the city, and saw his merry self emerge, full of vibrant youth and high spirits. In turn I found my self-consciousness falling away in their company. I was as open with them as I was closed-off with the Beauforts, more myself than I had ever been, even in those first wonderful weeks of travelling with Gloria, for with her I had always had a vague fear of doing something to incite her disapproval.

Sometimes Gloria joined us in our wanderings, and she was the golden centre of those times as much as she had been in Florence or Nice or Paris, but often she chose to stay in. I knew she was still deeply troubled by what had happened at the hospital, but I had no clear idea of how to help her, how to explain that though she may have failed some great test she had set herself, most people would not judge her harshly for displaying a sign of human weakness, and some, like Violet, would perhaps like her better for her failings. Jerry also joined us from time to time, and I came to know him as a cheerful, easy-going companion, who could always be depended on to say something to lighten the most serious mood, sometimes intentionally, sometimes not.

There was a ruined mill some way within the woods, a place of dark corners and crumbling damp stones, where we often went, bringing lunch with us, or books to read aloud to each other in the shadows of the mouldering walls. Thanks in great part to the endless curiosity of Mr. Bertram, his interest in and love of all forms of learning, the Ashford library was enormous, completely covering all four walls of the largest room of the house. From that collection we selected whatever struck our fancy, and I found that reading The Mill on the Floss within the ruins of an actual mill buried in woods reminiscent of the Red Deeps, surrounded everywhere by the sound of water, it took more complete control of my imagination than it ever could have within the confines of a house. There, we caught the spirit of it. There, it lived.

The sixth day brought an end to Perry's time away from London, and we said our good-byes sadly, though we knew he would return before long. That afternoon, after he had gone, Violet and I went out to the ruin and finished what remained of The Mill on the Floss, I reading until hoarseness took me, then passing the book to Violet and so on until we came to the end. On our return, I went up to the room Gloria and I shared with Cyryl and Haline (Violet had a small attic room she loved where she had slept in her childhood) and found Gloria there, putting the wardrobe in order. The room was large, and before our arrival a curtain had been hung down the middle, separating our half from that of the twins so that we all had at least some measure of privacy.

I had not had much opportunity to speak to Gloria alone since the incident at the London pub almost a week before. Our days had been full, and at night we had tumbled wearily into bed, grateful for sleep. Perhaps out of awkwardness we were both avoiding any more than casual conversation.

Our bags were still half packed, though we had been provided with a wardrobe and dresser, and Gloria was in the process of organising the remainder of her things. I joined her, pulling skirts and blouses from my suitcase, shaking them out and hanging them up. She looked round at me and smiled, but said nothing, and her smile still seemed sad to me. I felt a pang of guilt for spending so much time away from her with Violet and Perry, though I told myself that she had had every opportunity to accompany us on any of our excursions. I had never before really felt that she needed me. With her magnetism, her beauty, her engaging presence, I had never thought of her as needing anybody, but now...I didn't know what to do. I was afraid to approach her.

This awkward silence went on for several more minutes. I had my back to Gloria as I sorted through my stockings and put things away into drawers. When I turned, she had pulled something out of her suitcase and was sitting on the edge of her bed looking at it. It was her portrait from Florence.

Mine was still in my bag. I pulled it out and went to sit next to her. It was a conversational opening.

"We never did exchange them," I said.

"No point now," she said shortly. "We will probably be here for a while." From the way she said it I couldn't tell if she liked the prospect or not. Then she brightened a little.

"We should hang them on the wall," she said. "It will make it feel more like home."

There were three pictures hanging on our side of the room: a painting of Windsor Castle, a print of Waterhouse's "Miranda" and a faded photograph of a boy and girl sitting beside a tree in a field. The girl had long dark hair and a wistful expression and was looking down, away from the camera. The boy was looking forward boldly, laughing.

We hesitated for a moment in front of the pictures, not wanting to disarrange them too much to make way for our own, yet not overly eager to ask permission to bang two more holes in the wall.

"Do we take two of them down, or what?" asked Gloria, as much of herself as of me. "They might be family heirlooms or something, and we wouldn't want to stick family heirlooms in the back of the wardrobe."

I shook my head. I liked the splendour of Windsor Castle the least, for it seemed ostentatious, not fitting for Ashford at all. Miranda, looking out at the stormy ocean from the rocky shore of her island home, and the photograph of the boy and girl, were totally at home there. I could not think of moving them. I turned to look for somewhere else to put our portraits, and finally set mine down on top of the dresser.

"What do you think?" I asked Gloria. "At least it solves the wall-space problem."

"True," she agreed. "It's not perfect but it will have to do."

The dresser was set with its back to the curtain, so there was nothing to lean them against, but we solved this problem in the end by propping them against our hatboxes, which worked well enough, and we stood back to look at them with some satisfaction in our ingenuity.

"He really did a much better job on yours," said Gloria.

I shrugged. "He did yours first. Maybe it takes a little while for inspiration to hit."

We were still standing there in the most companionable silence I'd experienced in her company since her return to England when I heard a knock on the open door and turned around to see Jerry waiting outside with a small bouquet of tiny white flowers in a little blue vase. Gloria started a little at the sight of him, and I could tell that apart from her surprise she was still not used to him, so I took it upon myself to smile at him and say, "Come in."

"Snowdrops," he said, setting the flowers down on the dresser. "I thought you might like some in your room, and Grandmother told me you were here and I could bring them up."

I thanked him gladly, touched by his thoughtfulness, and out of the corner of my eye I saw Gloria relax as she added her thanks to mine.

I don't think he heard us. He was transfixed by the portraits on the dresser.

"These are wonderful," he said, touching the edge of the frames reverently with one finger.

I was glad he liked them, though I thought his enthusiasm a little excessive.

"I try to paint a little myself," he said, then added a little shyly, "If you would like to see I will show you sometime, but I can never get the faces quite right. I think it's the colour I don't get, or maybe the shading." He pointed at my nose in the portrait, and Gloria's ear. "The shading here is perfect," he pointed at a curl of Gloria's painted hair "and that touch of Burnt Ogre -- it's genius!"

"What?" I was trying not to laugh.

"Burnt Ogre. It's a colour, isn't it?"

He was beginning to sound a little less certain. I heard Gloria whisper, "I think it's Burnt Ochre."

I let myself laugh, as I felt that my restraint was becoming too obvious, and said that I didn't know, but that I supposed a burnt ogre might be that colour. He stopped his perusal of the paintings and looked a little embarrassed, but only for a moment. He was laughing heartily at himself as he left the room, and I could hear him on his way downstairs, saying to himself, "A burnt ogre. It would be, wouldn't it? A burnt ogre."

19

Was it strange that I felt as though Ashford had been waiting for me? Life with my grandmother had been an extended visit with a beloved but formidable relative. Arriving at Ashford had been more like a real homecoming than anything I had experienced before. That spring was the most beautiful I had ever seen, and I found myself forgetting about the war and its horrors as I watched first the snowdrops, then the daffodils bud, bloom, and fade, saw the new leaves unfold on the trees, and spent hours wandering through the lush young grass of the garden beside the old sundial with its growth of emerald moss.

My time was not, of course, spent solely in meandering through the garden contemplating the seasons. The house was full, and most of us (Mrs. Creeley and Mrs. Beaufort excluded, as their arguments with each other left little time for household tasks) had regular work to do which kept us balanced.

Mrs. Creeley had volunteered me to work in the garden, citing my potato-digging experience, and though I could not help disliking her method of suggestion, I welcomed the task, for it put me out of doors with the smells of spring rain and freshly worked soil, working generally with no one but Mr. Bertram, with whom I welcomed the opportunity to improve my acquaintance.

My liking for Mr. Bertram could only increase with time. He was a genuine, compassionate, earthy sort of man. He liked to get his hands in the dirt. He loved all living creatures. He detested all forms of falsehood. He said little about himself, but this much made itself clear through his actions. Of course, he was not perfect. His temper could flash out quite suddenly if something or somebody offended his sense of right, he could not abide cauliflower in any form, and the only time I saw Lilly Bertram truly emerge from her bubble of dreamy existence was one March afternoon to scold her husband for leaving mud from his boots on the carpet.

In the garden we talked about plants, and he shared with me from his vast knowledge of herb legend and lore, and we arranged an imaginary quest for mandrakes as we dug up the beds in preparation for spring planting. I also became his secondary automotive assistant, after Jerry, who had been his primary helper ever since the vehicle had arrived at Ashford.

It was on a pleasant afternoon in the middle of April that Mr. Bertram said to me, "I should teach you to drive, Anna. It would be a useful thing for you to know, and a help to all of us. Besides, you spend enough time helping me with the old girl that you really ought to have some of the fun as well."

So our driving lessons began, and though I was nervous at first I found that it came to me much more easily than I had expected. We kept it a secret from everyone but Jerry, Violet, and Gloria, who all enjoyed the secret as much as we did. The lessons were conducted out of sight of the house, and no one let anything slip until the perfect moment, when I drove to Wells to pick Perry up from the station on the occasion of his next visit home in late July.

"I should have known he would have you driving in no time," he said with a laugh after the first look of surprise had worn off.

"Your father's a fool to let strange young women drive his car all over the countryside," was the cheerful remark of Chester Sedgewick, who happened to be passing on his way to the ticket office. "He'll regret it."

Perry glowered darkly at Chester's back for a few seconds, then told me he'd been craving a pastry the whole way from London and couldn't possibly venture the rest of the way home without one. He fell asleep on the way to the pastry shop, and I had just time enough to start feeling awkward. The joke had been well-played. It had been his father's idea and it had been successful, but now that it was over I felt like I had no business coming to pick Perry up. I was not family. I had not even known them for very long as knowing people goes. I felt a strange return of self-consciousness, as if my inner being were returning to the shy and silent passenger on the train to Florence, before I had met any of the Bertrams, before the war, before so many things.

I parked in front of the pastry shop and turned off the engine, then leaned my elbows on top of the steering wheel and stared unseeing at the shop's hanging sign, thinking, while I waited for Perry to wake up.

I didn't have to wait long. He was soon awake, and teasing me for not rousing him. This familiar treatment put me more at ease, though I think I was quieter than usual, for I caught him looking at me curiously from time to time, as though he knew that something was on my mind. He never asked me what I was thinking about -- he rarely pushed to know anything which anybody seemed at all unwilling to tell -- but he was very kind, entertaining me with talk of the people he met in London and tales of growing up at Ashford, and he bought us both coffee and pastries before we set out again on the drive home.

Once we were under way he asked me about Gloria. He had, it seemed, been concerned about her after he had left us the last time. Violet had told him in confidence the details of that last day in London and Gloria's eye-opening experience of the hospital.

"I hope she realises that her reaction doesn't make her weak," he said, "only human. The other reason I'm concerned is that I had a letter from Tristan a few days ago and he was asking me about her. It seems that before he left they had agreed to write, but he's only had one letter early on and then nothing."

I remembered then that Gloria had been receiving letters. I had never asked her who they were from, assuming they came from family and not considering it my place to ask anyway. Our friendship had improved of late, and I had felt that we were nearly back on our old footing, but the truth was our footing had always been that of cheerful companions in good fortune, not of confidants passing through trials together, and she had not spoken to me of Tristan since that day in the pub.

"I've been afraid to ask her," I said, rather amazed at my own honesty, though I should have remembered that Perry had always brought out my blunter side. "She hasn't said a word about any of that to me since it happened, and I don't think I have any right to pry."

Perry considered this for a while, then said, "Maybe she's embarrassed that you saw her in a weak moment. She seems to me like one of those people who likes to be seen as incredibly strong -- not that that's a problem. It only means that they become that much weaker when they are caught in a failing that they would never want to admit having, even to themselves."

It was a view of Gloria's personality that I had not really considered.

The sky had been clear when I started out, but by the time we left Wells the clouds began to move in and soon a light summer rain began to fall, pattering softly on the roof of the car with a gentle rhythm which made me feel sleepy.

Perry kept me awake and attentive for some time with his stories of working in the city and his news of the war, which had more reality for me than what I heard in the radio reports ever could. In exchange I gave him the news from Ashford: of how Cyryl had outgrown all his clothes in the space of two weeks, how Jerry had offended Mrs. Beaufort by wandering into her room early in the morning and accusing her of attacking the castle, how Violet and Gloria and I had resumed our Red Cross sewing.

"I don't think any of us really likes sewing," I said, "but it's something to do for the cause. Violet is best at it, of course, she's so careful." I hesitated. "I always wish though that I could do something to bring in some money. I don't want to be a burden on anyone. I know my Grandmother sends enough to support me, but I don't feel like I should accept it anymore -- not now when everyone needs to do their bit and help each other. I know I do things around the house and I try to make myself useful...but..." I bit my lip. I felt like I was saying too much, but now that the words had begun to flow I couldn't stop them. "I'll be twenty on my next birthday, in just a few months. It's almost two and a half years since we were in Italy. Do you remember that day in the train?"

There was a short silence before I looked over at Perry. He was asleep.

I made a noise to myself which I was glad nobody could hear, something halfway between a laugh and a sob. I didn't know whether I was more sad or relieved.

I decided that I was relieved, and that Narcolepsy did have upsides after all. Lucky Perry. I wished I could sleep. Through the now-heavy rain I caught sight of a dark object in the road right in front of the car. I swerved to avoid it and thought I had averted disaster when I heard a thud and the depressing sound of air rushing out of a tyre which usually signified a puncture.

20

The ridiculousness of it all! I laughed for a few seconds, then in shame leaned my arms on the steering wheel and cried -- then cried more at the stupidity of crying over a puncture. I had been in Paris for the declaration of war. I had seen wounded soldiers walking the streets of London with lost looks, as if the things they had seen had stolen their souls. I had escaped with others from the bombed-out husk of what used to be a house, and I had seen the wreckage of homes all over London. I had seen all these things, and I had wept little or not at all. And now, I was crying over a puncture because it made me look foolish. Did that make me weird or just incredibly selfish?

I started as I felt a hand on my shoulder. Perry was awake and looking at me with an expression of such concern that I felt worse for having caused it.

"What happened?" he asked, "What's wrong?"

"I...I think the tyre's punctured," I said, feeling sillier by the minute.

I think he was relieved that it was no worse. It must have been hard on him, waking up to find the car stopped and the driver in tears.

He surprised me by pulling out his rather rumpled pocket handkerchief and wiping my tears away with the edge of it.

"Well," he said, "there's only one way to tell. We'll have to get out and see how bad it is."

It was bad. The thing I had seen in the middle of the road proved to be a broken spring, which, no doubt, somebody else was now missing on their own car. I had swerved to avoid it, but not far enough, and it had sliced open the left front tyre of Mr. Bertram's beloved automobile. There were a few tools in the car, sufficient for small problems, but nothing to fix something so severe.

"I guess we'll just have to walk somewhere for help," Perry said, getting up from where we had both been squatting in the mud to assess the damage. He said it in his usual cheerful tone, but with my shame-heightened senses I thought I detected a hint of weariness, and felt another pang of guilt at the thought of such a homecoming for him. "Gurney Slade would be the closest town from here, but it's still quite a distance. I think the best thing would be to find the nearest house and see if anyone has a spare tyre they would be willing to let us borrow. If we're lucky, we'll also be able to phone Ashford and let them know what's happened."

We got the car pulled off to the side of the road and prepared for the walk. There was a small black umbrella in the back seat which Mr. Bertram always kept there for emergencies, and which kept my left side and Perry's right, but the whole of neither of us, dry as we walked.

If I had been less drowned in rainwater and self-pity I might have noticed the brilliant green of the sodden landscape, the ever-changing shades of grey in the dark clouds, the dramatic flashes of lightning, but it is only looking back that I see these things clearly, and remember their beauty, for at the time, in the condition of my thoughts, I saw without knowing that I saw.

There was silence between us as we walked at the side of the road. I was lost in my own thoughts, and perhaps he was as well.

At last we saw a glimmer of light from the window of a house a little distance from the road. It stood up firm and strong like an emblem of sanctuary against the shifting darkness of the roiling clouds with a sturdy home-look that cheered even my depressed spirits. Perry and I smiled through the raindrops at each other, then set off down a narrow lane leading toward the house.

I became nervous again as we approached it, though for different reasons. *Silly girl,* I thought, *can't you ever stop? Will you always be like this, thrown into anxiety by every new experience?* I suppose I had thought myself cured, because of the ease and comfort of my association with the Bertrams and the level of self-possession I had gained through the trials of living in war-rent London, but it seemed that the strength gained through one variety of trial, such as surviving a bombing raid, did not translate to knocking on a stranger's front door to ask for shelter and spare auto parts. In an odd way this thought helped me, for at least in those past cases I had triumphed, or at least fumbled through with some degree of outward serenity.

We had to knock five times and had almost given up when the door was opened by a skinny old man with a large nose sprouting wiry grey hairs. A diminutive old lady who reminded me of a praying mantis stood behind him and looked suspiciously out at us from behind her husband's elbow.

They didn't say anything, just looked at us. It was unnerving. I began, "We, uh, had a pu..." and then cravenly left Perry to finish.

He took up my dropped thread as smoothly as he had when he saved me in the train so long ago.

"We were on the road from Wells on our way to Nettlebridge when we had a problem with a puncture. Could we trouble you for the use of a telephone?"

The old man stared at us blankly and put his hand to his ear. The old woman poked him in the ribs and yelled at the side of his head, "They want to sell you an elephant. I don't know why. Tell them to go away."

The man's eyes widened until they seemed to take up his whole face, then he began waving his arms at us and yelling, "Go away, go away, no buying here, go away."

We were backing down the front steps and preparing to run for it and seek help elsewhere when we heard a sound from behind the old woman, inside the house, and a voice called loudly, "Stop your screaming, Father. What is this about?"

The voice was imperious, the voice of a ruler commanding a subject, not a child speaking to a father. The noise and arm-waving stopped immediately and the old couple stood aside. Coming forward from behind them I could see a form in a wheelchair. The voice was that of a young man, though the light coming from inside the house behind him prevented me from seeing his face. He was propelling himself forward impatiently, giving no attention to the carpets bunching under the chair's wheels or to the furniture close by on either side. I jumped as I saw an old vase on a side table tremble and almost fall as he pushed past it. The vase rocked in circles on its base like a top, and I found myself holding my breath until it slowed and eventually came to a stop.

He came forward into the light and my relief at his coming to our rescue was marred by the expression he wore as he looked at us. It was a bold, unabashed sneer. I wondered what right he had to look at us that way, as if we were nothing, as if, should he choose to be kind to us, it would be for some whim of his own, indulged not because he cared what happened to us, two fellow creatures though we were, but because it amused him to use his power.

He looked out at us with mocking eyes as we stood there on his doorstep, the rain still pouring down on us in sheets. Through all my years of feeling ill at ease in company, all the times I had struggled to find words, I had never felt so much at a loss as at that moment.

"What sort of trouble would prompt a young lady and--" he looked Perry up and down in an appraising way "--an *able-bodied* young man, to knock at a stranger's door on such a dreary evening?"

He had moved nearer to the doorway, and what light there was remaining in the sky fell on him and I saw what must have once been a very handsome face before the infliction of a long scar which crossed it diagonally from the top of his forehead on the right side to the base of his ear on the left, slashing across one dark-lashed eye-lid, though the blue eye beneath remained bright and aware, accusing. I shifted my eyes to escape the fierce expression of his gaze and found myself looking at the loose fabric of his trousers where his legs ought to have been.

My mind went blank. I felt no nausea or faintness, only a strange pain in my chest.

"You, girl!"

It took me a moment to realise that he was speaking to me. I had been looking at my feet, but when I recognised that I was being spoken to my head snapped up and I looked him in the eyes.

"You may come in for a moment and use the telephone," his voice was kinder as he spoke to me. "I have no quarrel with you. I lost my legs for people like you." The bitterness crept back by degrees. "Little enough thanks do I get."

He moved his chair aside with a jerk to open a way for me to enter. As I stepped over the threshold I realised that Perry remained standing below in the rain. I did not think he had moved so much as a finger since the wheelchair first appeared. I looked down at the figure beside me in the chair and said timidly, "Couldn't Perry come in out of the rain while I use the telephone?"

He returned my look, and his face was set in hard lines, though they were not for me. "Day after day we crouched in pouring rain like this in the trenches, through hot and cold, and slime that was combined rain and sweat and blood. It's only fair that one of our soft-living countrymen should undergo the same for five minutes."

I was no longer at a loss. I was angry. I found the telephone in the hallway. Not even thinking of what I did I phoned Ashford. I know I talked to Lilly, but I have no recollection of what I said, only that I was coherent enough for her to understand that we had had a puncture and would most likely not be returning that night. Strange that the explanation of the accident, which I had been dreading with such intensity a few minutes ago, barely troubled my thoughts.

I came back down the hall toward the front door slowly. Neither Perry nor the man in the wheelchair had moved. Only one thing had changed. The little umbrella, which Perry had been holding over us both, now lay on the ground at his feet. Rain drenched his head and shoulders and ran in rivulets down his face and off the tip of his nose.

I said nothing. I pushed past the chair without acknowledging its occupant, stalked down the stairs and, standing in front of Perry, looked him straight in the eye. There was nothing there that I thought ought to be, no anger, no self-pity, no defiance. I would not allow him to be humiliated any longer. I still could not speak but

Ashford

I took him by the arm and led him away down the lane without a backward glance.

We were halfway out to the main road when I realised I had left the umbrella behind. I did not go back for it.

Melanie Rose

21

When we stood out on the main road again I stopped and turned on Perry.

"Why didn't you say anything?" I demanded, nearly as angry at him as I had been at his tormenter. "You didn't say one word to explain yourself. You could have defended yourself. You just stood there. Why?" I suddenly found myself glad of the rain, for it camouflaged the tears that I could not repress.

"He was right."

"What?"

"He was right. They go through things on the front lines that the rest of us can't even imagine."

"But you couldn't go to the front lines. You couldn't. Violet told me. It wasn't your choice."

"That doesn't change the fact that I'm not there. I can't experience what they do. I can never know the pain they go through, the fear. The war keeps going on and on but there is nothing I can do to stop it."

"You have an important job with the government, even if it's not on the front lines."

"A job that could be filled just as well by any older man or cripple who is unable to serve his country in any other way."

He was looking out across the dripping grass of the sheep pastures with a look in his eyes that made my heart ache. Hardly knowing what I did I took his face between my hands and turned it so that he was looking straight into my eyes.

"You do what you are able to do in the best way you can possibly do it. That's all anyone can do. Your family depends on you. We all do. You mean more to your parents, and Violet and Tristan and your aunt and the twins and even the Beauforts and Gloria and me, than that man back there ever meant to anyone or ever will."

For several minutes we stood there, staring at each other, while pain and anger, amazement at my own boldness, along with something else I could not name, washed over me with the rain. The thunder growled, the lightening flashed, and the anger fell from me and splashed on the ground with the heavy drops. I lowered my eyes and moved my hands back to my sides. There was silence between us, stillness. Then Perry spoke.

"I don't think we'll be getting home tonight," he said. "We should find some shelter for the night. Then we can walk to Gurney Slade in the morning."

We did at last find shelter in an abandoned shepherd's hut out in the pastures. The roof leaked in places but it kept us more or less dry, and we were tired enough from the events of the day that the uncomfortable stones of the floor could not trouble either of us much. We did not speak any more of what had taken place, but the old comfort of our association had returned, with a difference that I sometimes thought was real and sometimes imagined, a difference I felt as a pain which tied my heart and soul together.

When I woke in the morning Perry was standing outside. The sky was clear. There were still late blackberries to be found in the hedges, and he had two little piles laid ready on the top of a nearby stile. I thought it was the best breakfast I had ever had. I remember very little of the walk to Gurney Slade, or what we did there, except that we found someone willing to sell us a spare tyre and drive us back out to where Mr. Bertram's automobile waited forlorn at the side of the road. Yes, I remember that, and I remember the poster I saw in the grocer's window. The rest is blank.

The family at Ashford welcomed us back with an enormous dinner, which, after our sweet but meagre breakfast, not to mention no lunch at all, was extremely welcome. I was relieved to find that nobody seemed to see the accident as being my fault, except Mrs. Creeley, who satisfied herself with merely mumbling indistinctly under her breath and giving Mr. Bertram significant looks which that worthy man completely ignored.

It was only when we had all finished eating and had pushed our chairs away from the table that I told them the idea which had slowly been working its way to the front of my mind.

"I want to join the Women's Land Army."

Nobody spoke for a while. They all seemed stunned with surprise. I was not the one who did these things. Such an act of zealous fervour might be expected of Gloria, with her flair and her impulsive wish to do great things. I was not Gloria, nor was I British, and thus I was not expected to have such strong feelings of nationality for a country other than that of my birth.

I tried to catch Perry's eye, but he was looking down at the table and frowning. I hoped that he did not disapprove. Probably he was still dwelling on the events of the night before.

To my surprise it was Mrs. Creeley who spoke first.

"I don't know what all you ninnies are thinking, sitting there not saying a word," she said. "It's a good idea. She'll work hard and stay out of mischief. It's better than if she were driving around getting punctures and staying out late drinking with soldiers on leave at the pub."

Everyone laughed then, for they all knew that I had never been down to the local pub alone at all, and when there in company had never had more than a pint of anything stronger than water. Mrs. Creeley's statement and everyone else's laughter gave me courage.

"I've been thinking of it for a while," I said, "and then I saw the recruiting poster in Gurney Slade today. I'd like to be able to help somehow, and they will pay me a little so that Grandmother won't have to send money anymore. Some of the girls work in farms and orchards, and there might even be some places nearby that would take me. I like working in the garden."

Jerry looked at me from across the table, and a slow smile spread across his sad-funny gnomish face. "The Beauty worked in the garden for a long time before she met the ugly Beast in the cursed castle -- and he turned into a prince."

Somehow that finalised it. If Jerry could make a fairy tale out of digging in the dirt, then there was nothing more to be said. I got up to clear the table and Cyryl said, "Does that mean Anna's a grown-up now?"

Everybody laughed, and Haline, who was the quieter twin, elbowed her brother, while Cyryl ignored her and continued to stare soberly around the table in search of an answer.

Mr. Bertram clapped the child on the back.

"Yes, Cyryl," he said. "That's exactly what it means."

Violet got up to help me with the clearing.

"Anna," she said quietly when we were in the kitchen "I'll be seventeen next summer, and then I'll be able to join too and help you. It's wonderful." She gave me her slow, shy smile, then added, "I think you should talk to Gloria though. She might find it hard."

I looked at her curiously. She was right of course, but...

"You're wondering why I care," she said. "I know. I haven't been able to hide from you that I don't like her very much. But I don't like to see people in pain, however I feel about them. And I'm selfish, too. I don't want you to think I'm an awful, jealous person. I don't dislike her so much, and she is beautiful and sweet, and it's not her fault what happened in London. I just...I think you should talk to her."

I knew I should. The group in the dining room was dispersing. I saw Gloria sit down at the piano and begin to play. I recognised the beginning of Beethoven's Moonlight Sonata. We all loved it, and soon everyone had gathered to listen. Outside, I heard the wind rising as the rain fell, and a strange feeling of restlessness came over me, born of the rush of the storm outside combined with the melodic notes of the piano. Suddenly I wanted nothing more than to escape from the house and join the elements, as if I could somehow mix with them and become part of the storm myself. Speaking to Gloria could wait until the next day. The first movement of the sonata ended. I knew my mind was in no state to appreciate the various intricacies of the second. I passed behind the Beauforts without attracting any attention and slipped out the door.

I hurried through the back garden and up to the summit of the low bare hill directly behind the house. The storm was drawing near to the height of its intensity. Though I could no longer hear the music from the house, I knew that the second movement would be ending and the wild intensity of the third beginning. The melody filled my head, crashing chords matching the storm and filling me with a strange ecstatic fire which rushed through me, sending a prickly feeling down my spine.

The thunder growled like a prowling tiger and a flash of lightening lit the sky for an instant, making the outline of the Harridge Woods stand out in striking relief against the dark roiling clouds.

In that moment I knew with a sort of brazen certainty that everything was approaching its right conclusion. What was the power of war to the powers of rain and wind and thunder? I held out my arms to the storm as I stood at the top of the hill, the wind whipping my sodden hair across my face, the chilly drops falling from my nose and chin and the tips of my fingers, and I laughed. The storm was breaking directly over my head, but I didn't care. It could not harm me in that time and place. I was its child, if only for that one instant. Tomorrow the world might fall apart, but today, this moment, all was well.

22

The next morning I went in to the Women's Land Army recruiting station in Wells with Mr. Bertram and, surprisingly, Mrs. Beaufort. I suspected that Mrs. Beaufort came less to support me and more for the prospect of an outing, but she was very kind on the occasion, patting my knee in what was clearly intended to be a comforting way and saying that she hoped the transport vehicles were clean.

The office was staffed by a severe woman of about fifty or so, with hard features and an intimidatingly businesslike air, and an older man who somehow managed to be both alarmingly friendly and incredibly dour at the same time.

"Hello, my dear," he said when I introduced myself. "So you want to help, do you? Very well then," he spoke slowly, much as if he had a mouth full of honey, and moved ponderously out from behind the desk to stand before a map which spread over most of the opposite wall. The map had pins stuck in it at various places, marking, I guessed, the farms and orchards and other places which were in need of help.

Mr. Bertram and Mrs Beaufort had left me there and gone their separate ways to take care of business of their own. I was glad. My courage, though always a flimsy thing, was strongest when there was nothing for me to hide behind.

The man called me over to the map. He sighed noisily, and the hanging flesh of his jowls trembled in a truly disturbing way that made me shudder. He was not fat, but there was no muscle about him and all his movements had the slow, heavy, plodding quality of the morbidly obese.

"Where are you from, my girl?"

I foolishly began to state the name of the Maine town where I had been brought up, then thought again and said, "Nettlebridge."

"Ah. I suppose you would like to find something in the area? It might be difficult you know. Many of our girls have to move away from home and stay elsewhere. Sometimes if the work is close enough we have a lorry that comes by and picks everyone up in the early morning and brings them back at night, but, hmmm…can't always happen you see… You should prepare yourself for having to be far away from home for long periods of time."

I was starting to feel depressed. It was impossible not to feel depressed standing there listening to him drone on in a monotone. I had known before that I might have to leave Ashford. I just wanted him to get on with it. Preferably in as few words as possible. And I didn't like the way he kept eyeing the northern tip of Scotland.

Just as he was starting in again with a cough and a "hem…hoi…" I was surprised to see the sharp-faced woman come around from behind the desk, take him by the elbow, and propel him towards the door.

"I'll take this from here, Lionel," she said briskly. "Why don't you go down to the Crown and have a pint. You look like you could use it."

At that suggestion he was out the door, moving faster than I had thought his form or mental state capable of.

The woman turned to me.

"There are two other girls from the Nettlebridge area who are working on a farm several miles west of here. Meet them in front of the Nettlebridge Inn at six o'clock Monday morning. You will be trained on the spot. Uniforms are in short supply but you should have yours in a week or two. For now, wear something you could run after sheep or operate a tractor in. Thank you."

She gave me a small, automatic smile, handed me a stack of papers, and nearly shoved me out the door. Abrupt, but it got the job done, and all things taken together I preferred her method to the man's.

I had to wait some time for my companions, for they had expected me to take longer in the office and of course had errands of their own, so I contented myself with wandering the street nearby, looking in shop windows and speculating on my new job.

The shop across the street had hats and umbrellas in the window. Remembering that Perry and I had left Mr. Bertram's emergency umbrella lying in the mud in front of a strange farm house, I crossed over and entered the shop. I had some money with me, though I rarely spent anything except to help replenish the Ashford larder. But I would be earning my own keep soon. I planned to write to my grandmother that afternoon and tell her of my plans and that she need not send any more money. The knowledge of this approaching release from dependence made me feel freer than usual, and I thought perhaps I would buy something else, maybe something for Gloria. I still needed to talk to her, and it would be nice to bring her a gift, if only to show that I had been thinking of her. Part of me thought that anyway. The other part knew that it was partly just the easy way out, because giving gifts was easier than talking. Perhaps I would get something for Violet as well. The twins would need nothing. Mrs. Beaufort was probably out at that moment buying them all the candy she could on wartime rations. Cyryl and Haline now represented the whole of her passion for refugee children, and the sweet manipulative urchins knew it.

I found the umbrella first. It was basic and black like the other had been, but larger and sturdier, an umbrella that might keep two whole people dry. My attention had been caught at first by an incredibly garish one in a blinding shade of green with puce blobs that might have been cherries. I had to laugh a little when I saw it, for it reminded me of the distant Mrs. Whildon, with her colourful clothing and hearty chortle, and brought back many memories of our meeting in Italy.

Between searching the shelves for gifts for Gloria and Violet and looking out the window at intervals to be sure I had not missed Mr. Bertram and Mrs. Beaufort, I had a difficult time keeping my mind focused on the task at hand. I had little trouble finding something for Gloria. She loved things of beauty, and she loved colour. The hats were all too expensive even for my current feeling of financial freedom, but I found a little blue scarf in a shade that I thought would set off her spectacular hair to perfection. Violet was more difficult. She had very few small vanities. She never seemed to want anything material. The longing in her eyes was always for something Beyond, something that none but she would ever see.

I smiled to myself a little ruefully. "And you," I whispered "are only beginning to guess what you long for, but I very much doubt that greater mental clarity on your part will make it any more likely."

I glanced up, suddenly self-conscious, and noticed the girl behind the counter looking away quickly. I must have seemed very odd, standing there in front of the scarf display talking to myself. Then I looked out the window and saw Mrs. Beaufort standing out on the street corner, peering about her anxiously, probably worried that I had gone off alone into the city and been run over by a villainous cab driver.

I hurried up to the front and put my purchases on the counter, then remembered that I had not yet found anything for Violet. In a sort of confused desperation I reacted out of instinct. There was a display of picture postcards near the door, including one showing the dome of St. Paul's Cathedral. I could just make out the railing at the top where I had stood once with Gloria and once with Violet, looking down at the city. It seemed a small but fitting gift.

"This one too," I said, laying it beside the umbrella and scarf.

Mrs. Beaufort, in predictable fashion, had indeed filled her pockets with candy for the twins, and was also in a very anxious state as to my whereabouts. I found it a little bizarre that she seemed to worry about me more on these days when there was least chance of danger, as if by fussing over me between times she could erase the fact that in a crisis she hid behind me like a frightened rabbit.

But worry was an intrinsic part of Mrs. Beaufort's nature. No sooner had I joined her and received her exclamations of relief than she began to fret over Mr. Bertram's whereabouts, and it became my task to lay her fears to rest by assurances of Mr. Bertram's capabilities, his superior knowledge of Wells, and the fact of his having had many things to do while we had had comparatively few. In times of war and upheaval we cling to very odd things, finding security in sturdy objects and unchanging things. Walls, roof, table, chair -- we love them for their solidity, and we love certain people for very much the same reasoning. Though my annoyance with Mrs. Beaufort remained, that day I felt, with some surprise, a hint of comfort in the sameness of our association. It was strange, to be sure, but there was something soothing in the idea that Mrs. Beaufort would always be Mrs. Beaufort, would never do anything unexpected, would never be much less well-intentioned or much more sensible than she was at that moment.

Though Mrs. Beaufort had prophesied that Mr. Bertram would keep us waiting on the street until the sun started going down and her hair turned grey with worry, he arrived only moments after I had joined her and as far as I could tell the number of grey hairs on her head remained unaltered. He asked all the questions Mrs. Beaufort (in her worry) had forgotten to ask about my visit to the office, and when I had told him he nodded briskly.

"I was afraid you might get stuck with old Sedgewick," he said, and then added in answer to my questioning gaze, "Lionel Sedgewick. You've seen his son Chester on the train platform. Glad Miss Maria came to your rescue. Not too sociably inclined, but good at what she does, and she has almost a mania for fairness. She'll see you're treated well."

I remembered the long, lugubrious face of the younger Sedgewick, with its large nose and wilting moustache, and recalled what Perry had said about the family on the occasion of our arrival in Wells. Yes, I too was grateful for Miss Maria. She might be intimidating, but she was efficient, and she didn't make one feel patronised. I said so.

"Good girl." It was all he said in reply, but I felt that somehow in spite of the cloudy weather a cheerful sun had come out and turned its rays on me, and though I wasn't sure that what I had said deserved its glow I curled up on the seat of the car like a kitten and soaked up the beams. It was a gift of Mr. Bertram's, this benign, enveloping presence that pulled one in for apparently no reason and made one feel warm and safe no matter how the various difficulties of life tugged at one from outside. It was a natural gift that he seemed to have no knowledge of, and he had passed it on to his son.

But thinking of Perry this time brought on thoughts of the last few days, and I was not ready to bring them out into the light and examine them. They still confused me, and I preferred for the moment to have them remain where they were, haunting the background of my mind with their vague associations of pain and pleasure. Would someone else, looking from the outside, say that I was falling in love? Perhaps, and perhaps I was blind not to think the same. In my defence let me only say that I had lived a very sheltered life with my grandmother, leaving shortly after my seventeenth birthday to travel with the Beauforts, whose company did not offer many openings for romantic education. Thus, I had not learned by this, my nineteenth year, to associate a queasy feeling and a pain like a hand squeezing my heart with the love of which the poets sang. I was grateful to him. I liked him a great deal. I respected him. I pitied his situation. He was much older than I. It felt presumptuous to think more, so I left the ache in my heart and my queasy stomach to themselves and forced my mind into other channels.

Melanie Rose

Ashford

23

I still hesitated over talking to Gloria. I didn't know what to say or how to say it, but had decided that I would keep putting it off forever if I waited for the right words to come to me ahead of time. I would give her the scarf, and let the words come as they may.

Luck was with me. We arrived back at Ashford after the family had lunched, and found Gloria in the orchard. Allowing Mr. Bertram and Mrs. Beaufort to hurry on ahead of me and console their empty stomachs with the remains of the lunch, I stayed behind, telling my own growling stomach that it could wait for tea, and joined my friend.

"How was it?" she asked, smiling at me as we turned to walk down the drive together. Her smile was genuine, but it fled very quickly and did not touch her eyes.

"Frightening," I said, "but not terrible." And I told her about Lionel Sedgewick and Miss Maria and my appointment for Monday morning, as well as about Mrs. Beaufort's worries, which brought the desired amusement to her face, though only for a brief space.

"I brought you something," I said, and pulled the scarf from the small bag I still carried. I had left the umbrella in the car, and Violet's postcard I folded up in the bag and tucked into the inside pocket of my jacket.

"It's beautiful," she said, "and so soft. Thank you Anna. You didn't have to."

"I know," I answered, pleased by her pleasure in the gift. "I'll be working soon, and earning my own keep. I'm writing to Grandmother this afternoon to tell her to stop sending money, and I felt like making a little display of my new independence."

We had stopped in our walk and I took the scarf from her hands and tied it on over her beautiful hair.

"There," I said. "Perfect."

We walked a little longer in silence. I was inwardly preparing myself to ask her about Tristan, though the method of asking had still not come to me. But as it turned out there was no need for me to say anything. The silence only lasted a little while longer.

"I rather envy you right now," Gloria said. "I wanted to be the brave one, you know, doing a great thing for the cause, making everyone proud. Instead I'm the weak one, the one who couldn't handle the sight of injured men and had to run away, while you go to join the Land Girls. I could join too. I could, but I won't, because I don't want to just follow in your footsteps. I wanted to be the one who took the risk and had the adventure, and because I can't I will sit at home and watch everyone else do things. It's pathetic. I know it is. Everyone thinks so. I couldn't even bring myself to reply to Tristan's letters after what happened at the hospital, because I knew he would be ashamed of me. I'm ashamed of myself. He flies missions over Germany. He sees his friends shot down. And I can't even sit at the bedside of an injured soldier without fainting."

"Tristan wouldn't be ashamed of you," I said. "Everybody has a weakness. You know, Mr. Bertram told me a few days ago that he's afraid of spiders. And Perry..." I told her briefly of our encounter with the crippled young man. "I think he punishes himself every day for what he sees as his weakness, even though it is something that he has no control over. No one who knows what his trouble is blames him. You can't expect to be the only one without weakness, and I think--" I drew in my breath "--I think that it's rather selfish of you to not reply to Tristan's letters, and make him worry about you, just because you can't face up to being human like the rest of us."

She stared at me in astonishment.

"You really have changed," she said. "You were so timid when we met in Florence, always deferring to me for what to do or where to go. Now you're going on the Land, and telling me off for not being more forthright."

"I'm sorry," I said, ashamed of my outburst. I had meant to be sympathetic, not accusatory. "I had no right to say that."

She was quiet for a moment, then surprised me by saying, "You may not have had the right a year ago. I think you do now. I can't say I'll act on what you said. But I can't hold it against you, though I have to admit a part of me would like to. Let's not talk about it any more now. The air is cleared. Let's walk to the mill and pretend the war is over."

I agreed gladly, surprised at how painless our conversation had been considering the state of my mind leading up to it.

We walked to the ruined mill, talking of other things -- small things which were not related in any way to the war -- patterns in the clouds, the damp smell of leaves, how much the twins had grown in the last few months, and how Mr. Beaufort's bald spot had spread since our first meeting.

"I like this place," said Gloria, looking around at the surrounding trees, the flowing stream, and the dark, moss-covered walls that still, in spite of their state of decay, exuded an impression of strength and deep-rooted solidity. "I like it, but sometimes it makes me angry. It sounds strange to say it aloud, but everything seems so calm and unmoving. It's been here for so long, the house, or this mill. We all grow and change and are born and die or laugh or cry and break our hearts and these places just stay, with their ancient ghosts. I know it sounds silly, but at home it's different. Our house was built by my grandparents, and I always felt before that that gave it some great lineage, but this goes completely beyond any of that. Our house still feels shapeable. Its personality could be changed, if you can call it that. It would care if something happened to us. At Ashford I feel that even if we all died it would stay the same. Sure, the garden would get even wilder and the drive would be overgrown, but the house would have the same feel, the same sense of...I don't know...forever."

She stopped, having run out of words.

"That's what I like about it," I said. "I don't think it feels that way because it doesn't matter what happens to us, but just because there have been so many lifetimes building upon each other to make it what it is that now it changes very slowly. I find it rather comforting to think that whatever happens to us now there will still be places that feel serene and quiet, where things don't change easily. And I like to think that somehow all the lives that have been lived here before us are guiding us on. It helps me not feel alone. If there are ghosts at Ashford they are friendly ones. I don't know why, but I know I belong here like I never belonged at home. I love it in a way I never thought I could love a place."

She said nothing, but put her arm around my shoulders and together we sat on a pile of fallen masonry, keeping silent company with the ghosts, and I felt like one small strand of a large web, one brick in a huge pyramid, tiny yet essential. It gave me a restful feeling, but I felt Gloria shiver next to me. I could feel her fear and unrest as a distant shout, a call which a corner of my mind answered with its own hint of trembling before it was drowned by the greater silence.

The air was turning crisp in the early autumn evening by the time my stomach realised that it had not only missed lunch, but tea as well. We rose and turned homeward, and when we reached the front door of the house we both paused on the doorstep in spite of the chill to pay a last silent tribute to the darkening sky.

Melanie Rose

24

Monday morning found me waiting nervously for the two other girls and the lorry in front of the Nettlebridge Inn. I had forced myself to eat breakfast, knowing that the work would most likely be difficult and taxing, and had forced myself to give everyone a smiling and confident farewell, but both had stuck in my throat a bit. Lilly Bertram, in one of her rare outbreaks of practicality, had insisted on packing a lunch for me, but in characteristic form had forgotten the purpose of it part-way through and had turned it into an artistic masterpiece of fragile pastry and cream which would have looked very well on a tea-table but which I feared would seem out of place in an orchard or out in the fields, and I wanted so desperately not to make a fool of myself that first day.

I had said good-bye to the rest of the household in the kitchen, and they had all wished me the best of luck. The twins had both hugged my knees, pulling a little in opposite directions so that I almost fell over until I was rescued by Mr. Bertram. I doubted that they really knew what was going on, yet they clearly understood that it was something at least semi-momentous. Everyone was very kind, and Mrs. Beaufort called me her dear for the tenth time that morning, though it was still early, but as I turned to leave it was Perry I saw, looking at me over the heads of everyone else to give me one small smile, one brief, encouraging nod, and I felt as if he had thrown me a rope. It was a line I held fast to, almost without knowing what it was to which I was clinging, throughout the day, and it was only in the evening, riding back in the lorry at the end of an exhausting day of new experiences, that I remembered that Perry had thrown it to me that morning, that without saying a word he had given me my courage, and I thought of our first meeting on the train, and laughed to recall that he had reminded me of my dear, old, silly Uncle Nicholas. It was so strange to think of now.

I waited in front of the inn that morning for nearly half an hour before anyone else arrived, and then it was one lone female creature who came skipping down the hill from the opposite end of the village, her mass of unkempt dark curls bouncing. She had a plump, jolly face with a turned up nose and a light dusting of freckles, a short strong body clad in trousers that were much too long for her and a voluminous red sweater, and she was swinging her lunch sack about in one hand in such a careless way that it made me fear for its contents. When she spoke, only seconds after coming to a stop beside me, her voice had a Scottish lilt.

"Hello," she said. "Are you one of the other girls? Are you waiting for the lorry? Yes? Good. I really didn't want to wait alone, you see. I must have someone to talk to or I nearly go mad, you know. They all avoid me at home so then I talk to myself and that does get tiring, because you can never surprise yourself with your own answers. Have you noticed that? I like being surprised, too, but I can never think of something that's shocking enough to surprise myself. I'm Gwen, by the way, Gwen Gordon. My family is really from Scotland. Well, you probably guessed that, but you couldn't possibly guess how we got here. Well, it's not really all that exciting. You see, my mum's dead, and then my dad got his war job in London, so we came down here and now I'm living with my cousins. They don't know what to do with me, you know, proper English and all that. I tell them the Scots have always been scrappy and I'm proud of it, but they just look at me in horror. I'm really excited about going on the Land, just to get out of the house, and they're all glad that I'm going because it gets me out of their way, so it's a good thing for everyone, you know. I like you. I think we'll be very good friends, don't you? Now what's your name? Does your family live here? Do you have any crazy relatives you could tell me about, or are they all dark family secrets? If they are, please tell me anyway."

I found myself laughing in spite of everything, and, so that the perfect friendship she foresaw for us should not have a completely one-sided foundation, I told her my name, where I was from, and that I was living at Ashford for the present. I refrained from spilling any dark family secrets, but I had given her enough information to enable her to carry on the conversation quite comfortably by herself for another forty minutes, as I am sure she would have if she had not been interrupted by the arrival of the lorry, as well as the approach of another girl, this one very neat and very serious, and completely impervious to Gwen's attempt to strike up a conversation.

I was surprised, and rather disappointed, to see Lionel Sedgewick climb down from the driver's seat of the lorry and direct us all to get in. He hemmed and hummed about, told us we were brave girls doing a great service for our country but that he didn't expect us to enjoy it, though he seemed to think his presence must be a great comfort to us. Gwen ignored him completely and started talking to me again, while the other girl, whose name turned out to be Susan, kept her eyes on his face but seemed to see and hear him no more than if she had been deaf and dumb. I could only wonder what the rest of the day would be like.

Luckily, the jowled patriarch of the Sedgewick clan had only come to give us a familiar face to greet us, that we might enter our strange new life without fear, and he left very quickly (as quickly as he ever did anything) after dropping us at the farm and introducing us to the owner, Mr. Trumple. No doubt the mournful grimace he gave us as he laboriously climbed back into the lorry was intended to be comforting.

Mr. Trumple was quite jolly as farmers at that time went, the probable result of being a single man with no children, no siblings, and very little contact with his neighbours. In meeting him I witnessed for the first time the more positive side of being alone in the world. You could lose neither family nor friends in the war if there were none of either to begin with.

The first priority was to get the crops in, and we worked at it all that day, with a short break for lunch. Gwen, after laughing heartily at the lunch Lilly Bertram had packed for me, suggested we share both her lunch and mine between us, so we made a good meal between us of thick lamb sandwiches and flaky pastry.

It was in the days and weeks which followed that things really began to fall into place. Gwen's talent for all things mechanical was discovered, as was her ability to keep talking at an exhausting speed (at least for those listening) even while lying on her back under a tractor. Susan was cast of a different mould. It was living things that she loved, not wires and gears, and she took the sheep and cows and poultry to herself with an affection that I was sure she never showed to a human.

Mr. Trumple was not able to discover any special gift in me, but he seemed pleased to find that I did not mind getting dirty, that I did not need to be taught to drive, and that he could give me nearly any ordinary task and return to find it completed well and speedily. I worked at many things, my body grew strong, my hands more sure of themselves, and the days passed quickly.

It was late in the year, one day when I was cleaning the cowshed and trying not to freeze in the cold blast coming through the chinks in the wall that the news came. It was Mr. Trumple himself who came running to find me, with Gwen following closely behind, though she, for once, remained perfectly silent and waited for Mr. Trumple to tell me the news himself.

Mr. Trumple wheezed and mopped his brow, for he was unused to running and his round face was very red. Then he looked at me, shook his head, and told me.

The Japanese had bombed Pearl Harbor. The Americans were in the war.

Melanie Rose

25

I really could not say how I felt, or which one of the many thoughts running through my head was predominant. I was sad and angry over the bombing, of course, so unexpected and cruel. I wondered what this would mean for the country of my birth, for my grandmother and her friends and neighbours. Yet at the same time I was glad that here were more allies, that here was a greater chance of putting a final stop to this terrible thing which had enveloped us all in such pain and anxiety.

I was grateful for the remainder of the day's work, for it kept my body busy while my mind went round in endless circles, and I toiled harder than usual, pushing my physical being to outrun the restless circling of my thoughts. Better to expend my nervous energy in useful labour than to wear a giant hole in the rug at Ashford with my pacing.

Gwen, after the initial shock wore off, returned to her usual loquacious self. She stayed behind in the cowshed with me after Mr. Trumple had gone, asking me many questions about the attack and how I felt about it, and what effect I thought it would have on the outcome of the war. Luckily for me she answered most of them herself, detailing her own imaginings of how I might be feeling on the occasion far more eloquently and at greater length than I ever could have done, and I was spared the task of articulating more than a few monosyllables. I reflected later that it was a good thing that Gwen was not particularly observant, for by the end of the day I was irritated enough with her, and tired enough in my own body and mind that I could no longer keep from showing my frustration with her. By the time we climbed back into the lorry to return to Nettlebridge I was ready to explode, and it was my physical exhaustion alone which kept me from it. To speak required energy I did not have, so I was silent.

Returning home to Ashford I found the house dark and silent. I tiptoed in the front door and shut it softly, feeling like Rip Van Winkle coming back to his home to find that he had slept the years away and everyone he had known was dead. I hung my coat and satchel on the hook by the door and walked slowly through the kitchen, listening. The candles had not been lit and the moon-shadows came freely through the windows like stealthy young wraiths, falling across the stone-flagged floor and playing over the walls.

At last I heard a noise, a strange noise, not what I expected. Laughter.

It was in the sitting room that I eventually found them, Jerry and his mother, though they did not seem to see me at all as I stood in the doorway. It was nothing particularly strange or hilarious which met my eyes as I looked into the room, only Lilly Bertram combing her younger son's hair -- parting it all on one side, or brushing it all to the front so that it hung over his eyes, or making it all stick up in the middle -- and laughing as she did so, while he laughed too, pleased with her pleasure.

I left them there without a word, glad that they had not seen me. Neither of them belonged to this world. There was no reason why they should suffer for its pain. Jerry lived within his fairy tales, and Lilly belonged in a world of things now forgotten, of quiet green meadows and mild drifting breezes. It was right, I thought, but I envied them still, for I belonged to this world which was falling apart, could do so little to heal it, and yet could not escape from it.

I walked slowly upstairs and began to hear other, less pleasant but more expected noises. Passing the half-open door of the Beauforts' bedroom I saw Mrs. Beaufort crumpled up on the bed in her accustomed state during a crisis -- hysteria -- and I saw Mr. Beaufort trying to calm her, while Cyryl and Haline stood by with wide eyes, calmer than she, occasionally reaching out a small hand to touch her.

I could do nothing there. No one else appeared to be home. I turned to enter the bedroom Gloria and I shared, but I didn't sit down or throw myself on the bed as I had thought I would. I stopped in front of the three pictures on the wall and stared at them without really seeing for a while, my mind absent from my body, going far away to places I could not remember afterwards. I stood there for several minutes, then turned to look at the bed and the chair and the soft blankets, stopped abruptly, turned, and went downstairs again to the kitchen instead.

Back in the kitchen I lit the candles and reanimated the dying fire, then put the kettle on for tea, struggling to keep back a certain unreasonable feeling of resentment and self-pity which was threatening me. It didn't seem fair that I should come back sore and tired at the end of the day to find the kitchen dark and cold and the only people at home completely oblivious to my presence. I told myself that the others were most likely gone for a good reason, and besides, it was not their responsibility to have all the comforts of life ready and waiting for me. But who ever said self-pity was logical?

However, my spirits soon returned with the warm glow of the fire, at least enough for me to think about some sort of supper. Having no notion of when the others might return I could not very well prepare anything hot, but something of the toasted bread and cheese variety I thought would do very well, though I shamelessly used the last of our cheese ration, and dressed up the meagre helpings as well as I could by spreading slices of bread with a generous share of Lilly Bertram's special recipe lemon curd. I made the tea and settled down to wait by the fire, my cup beside me and a copy of Ivanhoe open on my lap. I would not read it. The courage of Rebecca would shame me tonight, for I was afraid. The book, open before me, and the tea, were merely the trappings of a valour I did not possess.

It was only half an hour before the others arrived, bringing sound and movement to the quiet, still kitchen as they came clattering into it. Mr. Bertram, his mother, Mrs. Creeley, Gloria, Violet... I found myself looking for Perry, then remembered that he had gone back to London weeks before. He seemed such an integral part of the group before me that it never seemed quite complete in his absence.

It was Violet who saw me first. I had risen from my chair and set my book aside, but she came over and quietly put her arms around me. I was surprised, for she had never hugged me before, but the sudden warmth and genuine sympathy of the gesture did more to soothe my troubled mind and aching body than I could have believed possible.

"I see you've set supper ready, girl," was Mrs. Creeley's approving remark.

"You look tired, Anna," said Gloria. "You shouldn't have."

"Well," said Mr. Bertram "shall we gather the others and eat before Anna's efforts go stale?" He patted my shoulder.

I smiled at him a little weakly.

"I think," I said, "that perhaps Mrs. Beaufort would prefer to have her supper sent up."

Mrs. Creeley snorted.

"Very well then, we will send it up." It was old Mrs. Bertram speaking. "Violet, get it ready."

Violet set about preparing a tray, while Gloria went to find Lilly, Jerry, and the twins and tell them that supper was ready. Mrs. Creeley sat down at the table.

"Letitia," said her sister sharply. "You will please take the tray upstairs."

To my surprise, though she grumbled under her breath about respect due to age and being given orders by her own sister, Mrs. Creeley got up from her chair, took the tray from Violet and a moment later we heard her heavy tread, made heavier from irritation, ascending the stairs.

Old Mrs. Bertram turned to look at Violet and me and smiled, looking rather mischievous. I was oddly reminded of my first meeting with Mrs. Creeley, and the glint of amusement I had seen in her eyes then. It was the first time I had seen much similarity between the sisters.

"I never could stand to see old people taking their privileged state for granted," old Mrs. Bertram remarked serenely, "and I really do get a certain amount of wicked enjoyment out of putting Letitia in her place."

When we were all gathered round the table Mr. Bertram informed me that when I had arrived back at Ashford from the farm they had been down to hear the news on the pub's radio, the one in the Ashford kitchen having experienced difficulties.

There was nothing particularly encouraging to report. The harbour had been attacked, many lives had been lost, and another nation had entered the struggle that was swiftly spreading over the entire globe. Britain, more precipitate in her actions than her more cautious, though formerly rebellious offspring, had instantly declared war on Japan as well. We were all bound up in it, and there was no escape for any of us.

26

I received a further blow the following day, when Miss Maria came out to the farm to tell me they were sending me away to work elsewhere. In the middle of winter there was little left for me to do where I was. Gwen and Susan could stay, for the sheep and the machines still needed their nurses, but I would not be necessary until the spring planting came on, if then.

I reflected later that I was very glad it was Miss Maria who had come to tell me. She brought it up quickly, with no avoidance, no insincere sympathy, just a plain statement of facts, with none of the pointless additions which "Old Sedge" as Gwen called him, would have judged to be indispensable. She told me where I would go for training, several counties to the North, what my job was to be, poisoning rats, and when I would leave, in four days. There was a hostel there where I would live with a few other girls.

I could not pretend to be thrilled over this coming change, but there was something in Miss Maria's no-nonsense manner and strict adherence to duty, which made one accept even unwelcome changes in spite of oneself. There is just a chance that I would have pleaded with the morosely kind Old Sedge to let me remain close to Ashford, but there would be no pleading with Miss Maria, no debasing myself before dignity such as hers. Without saying a word she held me to something higher.

The verdict at Ashford was mixed over my going. Mrs. Creeley said she approved of anything which would keep me in a state of usefulness and out of mischief. Mrs. Beaufort, still a little hysterical, reverted to tears again though she said at least I wasn't going under cover to France like so many girls who never came back, while Mr. Beaufort hoped aloud that they would feed me well at the hostel. Mr. Bertram spoke for most of the family when he said that they would miss me but that they were proud I was going. Gloria said she wished I wasn't going to poison rats, and Jerry informed me that it was usually the young men in fairy tales who went on quests to seek their fortunes, but that it occasionally took a journey for the girl to find out that she was a princess. Jerry then went away happy, content with his notion that I would come back royalty.

Violet said nothing during the family conclave, but later when I was alone in my room trying to think about packing and everyone else was downstairs challenging each other to a new board game called The Superman Speed Game, she crept up the stairs and knocked at the open door.

"Who's winning?" I asked. It was a silly thing Perry had brought home from London on his last visit as a joke, but to the amusement of all us younger set our elders had taken to it with a passion. Mrs. Creeley and Mrs. Beaufort were especially keen on it, and vied with each other with unswerving dedication. It was an amusing spectacle to watch, and usually I followed their progress with as much enjoyment as anyone, but that night I could not feel the usual enthusiasm and had retreated upstairs.

Violet sat down beside me on the edge of the bed.

"Grandmother was just ahead when I left," she said, "but Uncle was coming up close. Mrs. Beaufort isn't doing too well, but she's blaming it on the pawns."

Ashford

I smiled. I could imagine everything going on downstairs, and found myself wondering if I would be able to see it all so clearly in my head when I was miles away.

Violet interrupted my thoughts.

"You do know I'll miss you?" she said. "I'm afraid that I haven't been very good at showing it, but I do like you, a lot. It's always hard for me to say things -- so much easier to just do things, clean things, get things for people -- but I want you to know, for sure, before you leave. It's been wonderful having you here, especially with Tristan gone, and I feel like you're my sister, and I'll try to like Gloria as much as you do, because I think I love you."

The last part came out all in one breath and ended in a gasp. I could see her hands shaking in her lap but pretended not to because I knew she would be self-conscious about it. We were more alike than either of us had thought at first, that was certain. I had to say something.

"Yes," I said, "I know. At least, I do now, but I think I suspected before, and I love you like a sister too. I think it started that day at St. Paul's, but Ashford completed it."

I remembered then that I had never given her the postcard I had bought for her that day in town. I pulled it out now and handed it to her.

"I bought it a while ago," I said. "Then I forgot to give it to you."

"Thank you."

She said nothing else, just gave a slow little smile, and we sat there in comfortable silence together until the entrance of the twins erased all chance of quiet.

It was on the last day, as I stood in my room looking at my packed suitcase, that Mr. Bertram came to find me. He had said little about my going, but had been his usual kind, steady self, and had made the last days of my time at Ashford memorable in so many ways. They were small things, and I could not recall afterwards what they were, not to name or number them, but they were everywhere, in the sights and smells, in every moment of those days.

He came and stood in the doorway, smiling a little awkwardly, like someone who has something to say but doesn't quite know how to begin. Again, as he had the first time I met him, he reminded me of Perry.

He came a little farther into the room, then seemed to notice the pictures on the wall for the first time. He stopped to examine them, and I joined him in front of the wall on which they hung.

"I haven't been in this room in a very long time," he said after a few minutes. He pointed at the painting of Windsor castle. "My aunt painted that, you know. She used to have a great hankering to be an artist, when she was younger."

"Really?" It was all I could think to say. The idea of Mrs. Creeley being an artist baffled me, though it seemed right somehow. The straight lines, the almost harsh correctness of it, were like her.

Since we were discussing pictures, I asked him about the boy and girl in the photograph.

"Who were they?"

He looked surprised, then a little rueful.

"I guess we've both changed a great deal, though Lilly still looks like that to me. She was always a wistful-looking thing, and I adored her, even when we were children. The day she said she'd marry me I nearly died of shock, but she was always the one. She was the answer to my question."

I didn't ask what he meant. He seemed to have temporarily forgotten my existence.

After a few minutes he blinked and came back to me.

"I didn't mean to come in here and tell you my life story, Anna. I wanted to tell you that we will all miss you, even Aunt Creeley, though she'd be the last one to let you know it so it's up to me. I wanted to let you know that you'll always have a home here at Ashford, and by always I really mean always. Even when this blasted war is over and everything returns to some semblance of normality, we would all be overjoyed for you to come back to us."

"Thank you."

I thought of my grandmother far away, of her strict kindness, of her house that was the closest thing to home I had known before Ashford, and which was yet no home at all. I hardly knew how I had come here. It was always small steps, chance meetings, threatening catastrophes. A fury had blown me here, it seemed, a pursuing tiger, but it didn't matter how I had come. I was home.

I had found home, but in a matter of hours I had to leave it again, and I left in the midst of a flurry of snow. Everyone was very kind, and they all came to the station to see me off. Mrs. Beaufort cried, of course, but everyone else was smiling as the train pulled away from the platform to give me a good send-off, and I worked to memorise my last sight of them. The twins clutched Mrs. Beaufort's hands and tried to calm her while Mr. Beaufort stood with his hand on her shoulder. The large white flakes of snow were tangled in Gloria's brilliant hair, sparkling like gems that had fallen there. Violet was wrapped in an old coat of Tristan's, so much too big for her that her tiny frame was completely lost in it. Mr. Bertram stood between Mrs. Creeley and his mother, his younger son with him, and his wife, her dark hair falling loose around her shoulders, framing her face and its large dark eyes with their look of distant remembering.

There was one figure missing from the group, but I put him there in my mind, standing beside his mother, saying good-bye. He was still in London. He probably didn't even know I was leaving yet, and who knew what difference it would make to him if he did, but I saw him still. His hair would be standing up on end, as it had on the train to Florence when he had pulled it while he read the paper, and there would be snowflakes in it.

27

I was sent to training first, in a smallish industrial town to the North, which left little imprint upon my imagination apart from that of noise and dirt and the smell of rat poison. We were trained by a very brusque older woman whose warty countenance brought to mind the Salem Witch Trials, and whose large, rough hands were often rubbed together when she was explaining things to us, making a loud rasping noise reminiscent of the rats themselves scuttling around a barn floor. She was very fond of drawing parallels between us and the soldiers, between the rats and the Germans, between our poisons and our military's missiles; in short, between all aspects of our job and that of the boys at the front. She seemed determined to make us the most disciplined, deadly unit in His Majesty's service, and to do so in the allotted fortnight of our training. We called her The Sergeant among ourselves and forgot her real name, and under her command we spent a fortnight of little sleep and intense work before we were divided into teams and sent off in different directions to be a credit to her teaching.

The other girls training with me were pleasant enough, but though my self-confidence had grown since I had first arrived on English soil, we were not there together long enough for me to develop anything more than a congenial working acquaintanceship with any of them. I had learned how to make myself approachable. I had not yet learned how to approach. Thus, my friendliness consisted of waiting until I had something to reciprocate, and waiting required time.

At first I felt scrutinised by the others, though that may have been born out of a certainty that I would be scrutinised. I was the only American, and felt that I would seem an oddity, that they might not know whether to accept my efforts in spite of my nationality or to simply wonder what I was doing there.

It was easier once we had broken off into groups and moved on to our various work locations. Living in a hostel with three other girls, not to mention killing rodents for a living, did not perhaps make for the most comfortable circumstance, but it did promote a feeling of camaraderie between us all. After days spent together in barns and granaries, setting traps and gassing under the floorboards, questions regarding anyone's reasons for being there became irrelevant.

It was not a bad life in many ways, despite the unpleasantness of our task. The hostel, though bare, was warm in defiance of the cold without, and the girls were kind and full of fun. On our nights off we would wander down to the pub together and listen to the gossip of the town. There was a prisoners' camp nearby, and sometimes the news would be that someone had escaped, or been retaken, or that a new batch had been brought in. We sometimes saw the prisoners themselves being transported, Germans and Italians, and in the latter, though I told no one, I always saw the little painter from Florence, with his painting of Il Duce in its place of honour, and thought of his face and how it had brightened at my ignorant display of sympathy.

Gloria wrote to me often, as did Violet, with occasional notes included from the rest of the family, or pictures drawn by the twins, and I wrote weekly letters home to Ashford, telling of my life and work and asking for news. I addressed them to no one individual, but I began, slowly, to admit to myself that they were all for Perry. Though I knew that he was seldom at home it was he I imagined opening and reading them, and it was for him I included many details which would be lost on most of the others, things that I knew he would find interesting or amusing or touching.

Gwen wrote to me often as well, sharing many small anecdotes from work on the farm. Little things were rendered comical by her way of writing them, and I could never restrain my laughter when I read her letters, which brought on the curiosity of the other girls, until they awaited her letters as eagerly as I did, and begged me to read them aloud. She had discovered that Old Sedge's full name was Lionel Victor Sedgewick, so now she occasionally referred to him as Our Victorious Sedge, though she usually shortened his written name to OS or OVS to save time.

We were all given four days' leave at Christmas, and I spent a glorious time home at Ashford. Being away had sharpened my enjoyment of it all again, and even Mr. Beaufort's red face, Mrs. Beaufort's neuroticism, and Mrs. Creeley's ungracious remarks were welcome to me as a part of the divine mixture that made that place home. It was wonderful to walk into the kitchen and see Mrs. Beaufort swaying out of time to Ken "Snakehips" Johnson's "Blow Blow Thou Winter Wind" and crying into the wassail punch. Mrs. Beaufort always cried when Snakehips came on the radio. His death in a bombing raid had shocked everybody, but she had taken it as much to heart as if he had been a family member.

She always took things harder than anyone else, on principle, and however worked up anyone else became, always managed to work herself up a little bit more. Thus, while the rest of us uttered quite genuine moans over the death of Snakehips, she went into a conniption. She shed exactly one more tear than anyone else when I left for the North, and she rejoiced more eloquently than his own family when the news came that Tristan was coming home.

For Tristan was returning for a week. He had not taken leave in a very long while, and had at last been commanded to go home at Christmas. When I arrived at Ashford he had already been there for three days, and thus I missed what I had been so curious to see -- the meeting between him and Gloria. She had never told me whether she had or had not taken my advice and replied to his letters, and I imagined that in either case she would be nervous to see him again. By the time I arrived their behaviour towards each other was just what it had been before, and I was pleased to see the familiar flash in Gloria's eyes and the colour in her cheeks. It was difficult for us to spend much time alone together, with the house so full within and the weather too stormy without for much adventuring, but Gloria pulled me into a corner on the first evening of my return and let me know by a whisper in my ear (if I had any further doubts by then) that all was well.

It was a wonderful Christmas, and all was well in more ways than one. There were days spent by Gloria, Tristan, Perry, Violet and me by the fire, reading or talking or watching the flames, and there were days, during breaks in the weather, spent out of doors in the fresh cold air of the fields or forests. And all days were perfect, or seemed so. I stored up the memories in much the same way as a squirrel stores nuts, intending to take them out and look them over regularly once I returned to the hostel and the un-picturesque life of a rat-catcher.

The time passed much too quickly, spent as it was in trying to cram as much as we could into four days, and I was packing again much too soon. Tristan was to leave the same day, as was Perry, so that chilly December morning found the three of us waiting together in the kitchen to say good-bye. We took leave of everyone at once, except for Mr. Bertram, who was to drive us to the station. Mrs. Beaufort cried, and Mrs. Creeley bustled about as she always did when she didn't want anyone to know that she was upset. Then we all, in silent agreement, stood aside and pretended not to notice while Gloria and Tristan took leave of each other. Their farewell was that of lovers, and I turned away with a lump in my throat that came from sorrow and joy combined. The two are often mixed even in times of peace, but in those days of war they were almost never separated.

    I said good-bye to Mr. Bertram, Tristan and Perry on the train platform, with Chester Sedgewick leering morosely at us all from the ticket office. With such an audience my farewells fell flat on my lips, and I could give only silent replies to the words the others spoke to me, but I squeezed Mr. Bertram's hand when he gave it to me, shook Tristan's with a smile, and then, in a momentary burst of uncharacteristic courage, stood on my tiptoes and kissed Perry's cheek.

    I turned quickly away before I could see his face and hurried onto my train, tripping over my own feet in the process, and fifteen seconds later was mentally kicking myself for being so forward, but it was done, the train was pulling away and it was taking me with it.

    It would be a very long time before I saw Ashford again, or any of those I cared for so much, and before I did many things would change forever.

Melanie Rose

28

Returning to rat-catching after Christmas at Ashford was like returning to a dark cave after a sojourn in the sunlight. On my first day back we were sent out to a farm with a rat population as thick as gnats in a mire. Not frightened, furtive rats either, but big, mean rats who didn't seem to care at all for our size advantage or anything else, so long as they could keep their barn. It became a full-on war, with us yelling battle cries at the rats which would have made the Sergeant proud, and I was very glad that I had never had a great fear of rodents to overcome. One of the other girls, Ella, had, and I could see her hands trembling as she set her traps, though she bore it in true soldierly fashion and never said a word. I tried not to think of it all from the rats' point of view.

In the spring of that year the Americans came to set up a camp nearby, and things grew livelier, with music and dancing at the local pubs, and all the things which do come with introducing a new set of young men into a community whose own native sons went away to war long ago. Here I had a trump card in the eyes of my fellow rat-catchers, for I was American myself, and surely, they said, would relate better to these young men than they would, since they were not accustomed to American ways.

I did not tell them that I had always been a wallflower, or that large groups of young men had a power to frighten me that large hordes of rats did not, or that I was too absorbed in an older civilian Englishman with Narcolepsy to care for any dashing young American soldier. I only smiled, said that I would be happy to do what I could for them, and laughed within myself, for they believed me self-confident.

Actually, I was surprised by the outcome, for the soldiers, discovering that there was an American with the Land Girls, greeted me as a countrywoman and a sister, and I found myself, on our first meeting, the centre of attention for the first time in my life. It felt odd, as if I were taking something that didn't belong to me, and I wondered if that were what Gloria must feel, though her place at the centre of the room always came to her by right -- in my case I felt that I had usurped it.

I did my part by introducing my fellow rat-catchers, nodding and smiling when spoken to, and tapping my toes to the music whenever there was any. There very frequently was music, for many of the young men played instruments, and the girls were always more than willing to dance.

It was not my element, but it was jolly and lively and helped the time pass. Most of the young men were perfectly happy with my reticence, for it gave them ample opportunities to tell tales of their own, and I was often regaled with stories of battles and glory, though these soldiers were still rather green and had experienced little of the first and even less of the second. Perhaps, had they been more battle-hardened, they would have been less chatty about it. But then, in that case they probably would also have been less entertaining.

But even the casual friendship of these soldiers brought pain with it as time went on, for the war continued, and there was constant change within the camp. Every so often a group of soldiers would ship out, or a new batch arrive, and all too often we got the news that the Lieutenant I had laughed with a month before, or the Captain with whom Ella had danced, was dead or wounded. And the ones who did return had become more battle-hardened -- and less chatty.

It was a kind of sorrow I had not known before with my comparatively sheltered view of the war, and it tore at my heart in a way I could not have imagined. There was a hospital nearby where the wounded were brought in, and my fellow rat-catchers and I took to visiting it in the evenings when our work was done. We became almost surrogate nurses, for the hospital was short-staffed and what staff they had were often overworked and exhausted. We did the things that did not require training and thus freed the trained nurses and nurse's aids for other, more important tasks. We brought water, food, and extra blankets to the wounded. We sat beside them, held their hands when the pain became too great, and pretended not to see their tears. And then we smoothed out our worry lines and went to the pubs to cheer and encourage the new troops. It was a strange double life, but it was all we could do.

I did not write to them at Ashford about my extra work at the hospital, for I was worried that if Gloria heard about it would throw her back into depression about her own brief stint at a hospital, which I absolutely did not want. It had been so wonderful to see her well and happy again, and I wanted to see her that way still in my mind. It was the thought of those I loved most happy and well at Ashford, and my memories, faded though they were becoming, which kept my soul strong and my courage up in those days. I would do nothing to tarnish those images, nothing that would place a blot on their lives, even if the blot was only in my own thoughts of them. They would have their sorrows. I knew, and could not change, that fact. But their sorrows should not come about because of me. So I wrote glowing letters about my life, romanticising my work and telling of our new social engagements, until Gloria wrote that she quite envied me.

Christmas came again, and this time we were not allowed more than one free day. The war would not cease for Christmas and neither would we. No one was to go home, so it became our focus to make that one day as pleasant as effort could make it.

We planned a Christmas party for the evening, calling on all our acquaintances to issue invitations by word of mouth due to the scarcity of writing paper. It was to be held in the common room at one of the local inns, and we were there in the morning to set up and give everything its most festive appearance before returning to the hostel to change.

We had gone out at first light to cut boughs from a grove of holly trees which lined the East road into town not far from our hostel, and, before taking them all to the inn, had gone to the hospital to pin a sprig of holly at the head of each man's bed. One soldier, as I stood by him, reached out and touched my arm.

"You're having a party tonight?" he asked hoarsely.

"Yes," I answered, sitting down on the edge of his bed. He had a neck wound which made it hard for him to speak. Best, I thought, to let him speak softly.

"You have a party dress? A pretty one?"

I nodded. I was a little embarrassed by it, for I had scraped by on a fraction of my meagre income to afford it, and it felt like such a frivolous thing.

"You'll come here, tonight, at some point, to show me? None of us have seen a pretty girl in a nice dress in so long."

I could not refuse anything so simple to a wounded man. I had always been awkward about my appearance. Not that I thought myself ugly, but I had always been hesitant to be noticed, and the uniform of a

Land Girl, which I had worn nearly every day for over a year by that time, was built for function, not comeliness. But then, I had never thought of the thing from the angle this soldier presented it from before, as a gift. It did not seem a petty or frivolous thing in that light, if you made yourself attractive to cheer the eyes of a hurt or dying man; no more than setting a flower in a vase on the table beside him.

"I will," I said.

Melanie Rose

29

It was not many hours later that I stood before the looking glass at the hostel, putting the finishing touches to my evening dress. I was inordinately proud of it, for I had never had a real evening dress before and had saved somewhat fanatically from the time we decided to have the Christmas party to be able to afford it.

I turned in front of the mirror, enjoying the feel of the full taffeta skirt and the rustle of the petticoat beneath. It was the colour of butterscotch, warm and glowing, a bolder shade than I would have expected myself to choose, but I had known it was the one I wanted the moment I saw it. It had no sleeves, and it was taking me a while to get used to my own bare shoulders. I had no fine coat to go with it, for I would have had to save for another three months to acquire one, so my old rat-catcher's coat would have to do the job until we arrived at the inn. It seemed strangely fitting to me that I would not unveil my finery until the last moment, and then, when the evening was over, disappear into my tatters again like Cinderella at midnight. At least the coat had been washed, so that for one evening it would not bear with it the stench of rat poison.

The other girls were around me, for we all shared the one mirror. Ella, in a creation reminiscent of whipped cream and strawberries, twirled beside me. She had twisted her blonde hair into ringlets and looked like a happy little girl. The other two girls, Jen and Emily, were in green and black respectively -- the green of Jen's dress very vivid and striking with her chestnut hair, and the black of Emily's setting off her pale skin and dark hair to perfection.

I had told them about the wounded man and his request, and we had agreed to leave the party for a little while once it was underway to pay the promised visit.

We walked to the inn as the sun was sinking, and the brilliant golds and reds of a winter sunset were spreading across the sky. I would have loved to stop and admire it longer, but the chill was creeping in under my skirts, through my thin dress stockings. It was not a long walk, but it had been a cold day and our finery was not built for warmth, so we were very glad to leave the chill behind and enter the warm common room. A huge fire was blazing on the hearth and Mr. and Mrs. Barker, the innkeepers, were waiting for us in smiling welcome.

I had argued with the others for turning off the electric lights and using candles, and had won. I said it was because it would create a pleasant atmosphere, but I admit it was more of a nod to Ashford far away, where they would be having their Christmas chicken by the light of the traditional Ashford candles. There would be fresh holly, and there would be candles, and those two things would bring us that much closer in spirit.

Everything was ready long before it was time for anyone else to arrive, so the four of us rested at the bar with the first samples of Mrs. Barker's famous wassail punch, surveying our handiwork with pleasure. The arched rafters were hung with numerous holly boughs tied with red ribbons, and there were candles down the length of every table. It seemed to me like an image pulled out of history from several hundred years ago, when the old inn had been new-built. I could just imagine it, with some local lord presiding over the board, and a troupe of minstrels ready with their instruments. There was no lord now, but there was Mr. Barker beaming at us with his round cheerful face, and Mrs. Barker for his lady. There were no minstrels, but soon the soldiers would arrive, and some would bring their instruments and tonight we would have laughter and carol-singing enough to wake the spirits of the lord and lady and minstrels of old.

The first of the guests began to arrive, and soon the room filled. I was happier in this position than I generally was in crowds, for as one of the hostesses I had a great deal to do, and was not simply standing in a corner wanting the nerve to speak to someone. I wandered the room, keeping everyone supplied with punch and bestowing smiles. Smiles were simple and took little effort, and one soldier paid me the compliment of saying that I looked radiant. He was very young indeed, and had already had a great deal of punch for the time, yet that did not prevent me from feeling flattered by his attention.

When I was sure that nobody would be wanting more punch for a while, and that all was merry, I slipped into a corner by the fire and stood watching the festivities, thinking of the family at Ashford and wishing they could be there with me. It is embarrassing to admit, but I did have a small secret wish that they could see me like this, for one evening the princess of Jerry's imagination. It was with an idea of showing it to them all on my next visit that I agreed to pose for a photograph with the other girls and some of the soldiers, along with some of the nurses from the hospital who had managed to get the night off.

It was some hours before I remembered my promise to the soldiers, and the other girls were evasive when I mentioned walking to the hospital. It was too cold, Jen said, and we would already be walking back to the hostel in the dead of night. We would show them the photograph. Ella, who I had counted on most, was being thoroughly romanced by a dashing young Captain and had stars in her eyes.

After hesitating for a time I slipped back to the kitchen to say a quiet word to Mrs. Barker about where I was going, took down my rat-catcher's coat from its hook and wrapped my warm scarf around my neck. As an afterthought I pinned a sprig of holly in my hair and asked Mrs. Barker for a bottle or two of wassail punch.

Mrs. Barker, being a worthy and compassionate woman, loaded me up with three large bottles of the punch and a loaf of dark fruitcake studded with golden raisins. Then she patted my cheek in a motherly way and sent me off with a compassionate smile, saying,

"Make those poor boys forget their injuries for a little while, love."

I walked as quickly as I could through the frozen streets with my burdens, but even so my fingers were freezing by the time I reached the hospital. The head nurse received me kindly but hurriedly, as they were even more short-staffed than usual due to the absence of the nurses who had the night off. She had no objection to the punch or the fruitcake as long as it was spread evenly among the patients, and even allowed me to heat the punch on the stove in the hospital kitchen. Leaving my coat and scarf behind at the door I set about preparing the punch and fruitcake before making a few last-minute adjustments to my dress and, feeling slightly flushed, walking slowly into the main ward with a tray in one hand and a pitcher of punch in the other.

It was as I was passing between the beds, pouring a glass of punch here, handing out fruitcake there, that I realised the key to it all, the reason this thing was important. I, myself, had nothing to do with it. To these men, even those I had sat beside and comforted, I was not myself tonight but a symbol of something else, something larger and much more powerful. It was as an embodiment of what they fought for that I was important. It was an idea which I found encouraging and humbling at the same time. It took me out of the question entirely, a curious release. Stepping out of myself I was able to do what I would never before have thought possible, smile at these men with holiday cheer, show off my dress, and accept their admiration and expressions of gratitude with grace. It was not me. It was the greater symbol which had taken me over for that one evening.

I was still in the throes of this feeling of Something Greater, when the head nurse approached me a little apologetically.

"I wouldn't ask you under normal circumstances," she said, "but Private Simkins is going fast. He's been asking to see you. Calls you, 'The girl with the rough hands and the shy smile'."

Private Simkins was the man I had spoken with earlier that day, who had asked me to come. I had looked for him among the patients and had not seen him. So he was dying. Of course he would be in a different ward. I looked down at my hands. They were rough, most recently from handling the chemicals of our trade, but even from before, from the work I had done in gardens and orchards. I had scrubbed them well for the evening though. At least they were clean, not that it mattered.

I looked up at the head nurse, who was watching me anxiously.

"I will come," I said.

She took me down the hall and into another ward. It was quiet there, and still, but I thought the stillness had a chill in it.

The head nurse took me between the rows of beds to one by a window on the far side of the room.

Private Simkins was watching for us, and his eyes brightened as we came towards him.

"You came," he said weakly, smiling a little, "and you have holly in your hair. My mother always told me that holly kept evil away. Perhaps I won't be afraid to go if you are here."

I couldn't speak, but I sat beside him and he seemed to think that was enough. I don't know how the time passed, but it was in the wee hours of the morning that he opened his eyes for the last time and looked at me in silence. On a sudden impulse I reached out and gently touched the wound on his neck. There had been complications with it and it had begun to bleed afresh. I don't know why I did it, it only seemed the right thing to do at the time, but it appeared to calm him, and I left my hand there until the nurse, checking his pulse, informed me that he was gone.

Very slowly, feeling as though I was not in command of my own limbs, I took the holly sprig out of my hair and put it between the fingers of the dead man, ignoring his blood hardening on my hand.

I stood up and moved to the window while the nurses took care of the body, not seeing anything of the dark shadows without or the reflection of the scene within. I was still standing there twenty minutes later when I heard a voice from behind me pronounce my name. Shaking myself out of my trance, I turned, and to my surprise saw Mr. Beaufort.

He was staring at me as if he couldn't believe his eyes. I certainly must have been a sight, at the bedside of a dead man in an evening gown with blood on my hand, my hair in disarray and my face white with fatigue and tragedy, but the look was not all for me. His red face had a grief-stricken expression that I had never thought it could wear, and he approached me with a gentleness I had not known he possessed, and took my hand -- the clean one.

"Tristan is dead."

Melanie Rose

30

I wished I could faint. I wished I could cry. But I could do neither. I think my lack of an emotional response frightened Mr. Beaufort more than anything else, used as he was to the exaggerated feelings of his wife, and he gripped my hand tighter and led me to a chair which the head nurse kindly set ready. Once there he remained standing beside me with his hand on my shoulder, as if he was afraid to let go lest I should fade away.

"He was flying a mission over Germany," Mr. Beaufort told me "when his plane was shot down. They determined that no one could have survived." He paused for a moment, as if waiting for me to answer him. I didn't. He went on. "I stopped at the hostel to find you but you weren't there. The other girls said you hadn't come back from a party last night and I started to worry, but then one of them said you might still be here."

I nodded slowly, acknowledging his worry, but my mind was far away, at Ashford with Violet and Gloria, Mr. Bertram and Lilly, Jerry and the twins, and Perry. What must they all be feeling? Theirs was a pain I could not imagine, for though I had known and liked Tristan, I had not been sister or cousin or lover to him. It made it worse somehow that they had not found the body. Worse because of the false hope that would rise up only to be crushed by common sense. His plane had been shot down and its pieces scattered over Germany. No one could have survived. No one.

There was silence again. I wanted to know how the family was, how Gloria bore the news. I wanted to know the answers to my questions without having to ask. I wished, rather unreasonably, for Mr. Beaufort was doing his best, that Perry had come to tell me. He would have known what I was waiting to hear, would have known how to tell me, and I would not have had to go through the agony of dragging the words out.

Then remorse seized me. After all, Mr. Beaufort had come all the way from Ashford to tell me, had obviously taken the night train and had little sleep. There were dark shadows under his eyes, what remained of his hair was tousled, his usually red face pale. Why could I be a help and a symbol to a hospital full of wounded strangers and not to this familiar, inoffensive man beside me? I noticed for the first time how much older he looked than he had when we first set out on our tour of Europe. It seemed so long ago, so much longer than the three and a half years of its reality, and the whole of it, the time, the fear, the anxious waiting, had aged us all. I looked up from my lap and met the eyes of the man I had regarded with amusement and contempt for so long, and I found myself looking into the eyes of a comrade. The comedic element was still there, underneath, but the humanity and the need were uppermost.

I stood up and smoothed my dress.

"Come back to the hostel," I said, endeavouring to keep my voice from shaking. "You look like you could use a cup of coffee. They'll let me take a day off since you are here, and you can tell me more once we're both more comfortable."

Once we were outside Mr. Beaufort gave me his arm. I took it, not so much at first for the support it offered as for the comfort it would give him to believe that he was assisting me, but I found myself leaning on it more as we went along and I began to realise my own weariness.

Once we were back at the hostel and I had washed my hands and changed into my everyday clothes, I made coffee and Mr. Beaufort and I sat down at the kitchen table to drink it, accompanied by some muffins spread with a little marmalade. It seemed poor fare to me after the meals at Ashford, which old Mrs. Bertram and Lilly had made delicious by virtue of their great skill in spite of rationing, but it was all that I could find in the cupboard.

At last I put the question which had been haunting me.

"How is everyone at home?"

Mr. Beaufort did not answer at once. He sat for a moment staring at his coffee as he swirled it about in his cup, cleared his throat, looked at me, then looked down again.

"Mr. and Mrs. Bertram and Mr. Bertram's mother took it pretty hard at first, and poor Jerry didn't know what to think. It's impossible to tell what old Mrs. Creeley felt. I never know what she's thinking. It was very hard for everyone."

He paused again, and in spite of our new sympathy I wanted to shake him, for he had said as of yet nothing about either Violet or Gloria.

He cleared his throat again, and when he spoke it was very quietly.

"Miss Gloria and Violet are gone."

Melanie Rose

31

"Gone? Where?" I still barely grasped what he had said.

Mr. Beaufort sighed deeply and mopped his forehead with his handkerchief.

"To London," he said. "The morning after we heard about Tristan's death they came downstairs together and told us that they were going to London to pursue more active work with the Red Cross. They looked, both of them, like they hadn't slept a wink all night. We hoped that maybe they wrote to you. You were close to both of them, and we thought that maybe they would tell you what they wouldn't tell the rest of us. We're all worried that they'll try to go somewhere dangerous, and even though nobody says anything I know everyone's thinking of the last time Miss Gloria went to a hospital."

I could imagine them all when the news came, could feel their grief almost as keenly as I had felt my own. Mrs. Beaufort would have fallen at once into hysteria, doing her anxious husband the favour of keeping his grief at bay by distracting him with her own. Gloria would not have wept until she was alone in the safety of our old room, where the tears could fall unseen and unchecked. Violet alone would be dry-eyed through it all, her sorrow much deeper for the loss of her only brother than appeared from her lack of visible anguish, with nothing to soothe the burning of her dry eyes or the ache of her heart. It was not strange that both Gloria and

Violet would be thrown into action by the tragedy, I thought, though for completely different reasons. The strange thing was for them to each find an ally in the other, when their natures were so opposite, their minds and souls so alien. I was glad, if that word could be used, that they turned to each other rather than bearing everything alone.

I did my best to comfort Mr. Beaufort, telling him that I would let them know if I received a letter, and reassuring him that they would not have gone without some sort of plan, though I was having some difficulty giving myself the same assurance. Finally I reminded him that Perry was in London most of the time, and that with him they would always have a place to go if things did not turn out as they hoped.

After our meagre repast we fell into silence, and shortly thereafter Mr. Beaufort noticed his own exhaustion enough to seek a remedy by falling asleep on the sofa. He would leave on the evening train, and I found myself wishing he had longer to stay. While my concentration could be focused at least in part on calming his anxiety and keeping his fears for me at bay I had a great deal to do and think about. Once he was gone it would all come back. I would remember what I had just now pushed to the back of my mind, that not only had I lost a friend, but I had also watched by the bedside of a stranger as he drew his last breath. The two were connected for me, melding past and present, near and far into one mass of pain and horror like a leaden mass lying cold at the heart of the empty hull which was my body. From some distance in my mind a Frenchwoman wept for her two dead sons, and my heart cried for her loss as well as for mine.

I walked Mr. Beaufort to the train station in the late afternoon, he boarded the train and was gone. I was alone. Alone with my leaden mass and the ghosts of not two men but four, and I found myself speaking to them, reaching out to the dead for comfort because they suddenly seemed more real and present to me than the living.

Then the girls came home with their questions and concern, and the loneliness, instead of growing less, only became greater and more overwhelming, for in the presence of the living the nearness of the dead faded away but the nearness of the living was only that of the body, not of the soul. I answered their questions as concisely as I could, and left them as quickly as I was able in spite of their pressing invitation for me to join them for dinner at the inn. I had no appetite, I told them, and would be poor company in any case. I did not say that under the circumstances their presence only increased my feelings of desolation.

The next day work began again, and I was able to find some solace in the regularity of our routine, though I went about my work silently and seldom joined in the conversations of the others.

I also discontinued my evening visits to the hospital, at first because I felt that I could not bear it after the recent events, then later out of fear, though I felt guilty whenever the door of the hostel shut behind the others on their way there. They never questioned me, and were very kind, but I imagined what they must be thinking, and my overactive fancy made great what was little and increased my shame by dwelling on what I considered their thoughts of me might be.

I did at last receive a letter from Violet, with a short note from Gloria enclosed, to inform me that they were safe and well, and to apologise for not writing sooner. It was kindly written, in such a way as to allay my fears, yet I felt that it told me nothing.

They were in London. They were safe. As safe as could be expected. They were doing Red Cross work, though neither said exactly what that work was. They had seen Perry several times and he would take care of them if anything were to happen. I was not to worry, and I was requested to reassure the rest of the family at Ashford to the best of my ability.

I replied to the letter, asking for more information about their work, and assuring them that I understood their reasons for leaving, though it would be difficult to obey their instructions and not worry. London was still a war zone, after all, and I didn't know where in London they were or how dangerous their task was. I sent the letter to Perry's town address, knowing that he would pass it on to the girls for me, and included a brief note for him asking that he keep me informed of their welfare.

I did not expect a visit from him, but he came. One drippy evening in mid-February, when I returned from that day's rat-catching, he was waiting at the hostel. The place seemed full of an unaccustomed warmth as we came in the door and I felt his presence before I saw him -- felt it as a lightening, a restfulness, a serenity within myself that I had thought lost, gone into the next world with the men who had died. I knew that I had missed him, but I only knew how much when I saw him there. His familiar smile was just as ready, but not quite as I remembered it. It was, perhaps, a little sadder, but just as kind, just as all-encompassing, reaching out not only to me but to the girls with me so that we were all enveloped by it in spite of our end-of-the-day weariness. I altered the picture of him in my mind to add that new sadness to his smile, so that the portrait should be as accurate as it could be, then stepped forward to welcome him and introduce him to the others, feeling a little anxious underneath the serenity owing to my impulsiveness on the occasion of our last parting.

"I'm surprised to see you," I said, when we had sat down. The girls, after a few short minutes of polite conversation, left us alone together at the kitchen table and went to change out of their dirty rat-catching clothes. I wanted to change out of mine, for I felt mousier than usual in them, not to mention the surrounding pungent haze of poison fumes, but felt I must hear any urgent news he brought first. My thoughts, of course, went quickly to Violet and Gloria. Had anything happened to them? I asked him.

"No," he said, and I felt a great deal of the weight I had been carrying fall from me at his utterance of that monosyllable.

"They were very well when I left London," he said. "I don't hear much of their work, but I know that Violet is a nurse's aid, and Gloria does anything the Red Cross sees fit to ask of her. Is it so hard to believe that I would come to visit you just to see that you were well, without bringing bad news with me?"

It was hard for me to believe, but I didn't say so. Instead I mumbled something indistinct about everybody being on edge these days, just waiting for disaster, and that I was no different. It was true, so what matter if it were not the whole reason behind my anxiety?

"And how are you?" he asked, looking at me as if he could see into me and knew the answers before I gave them. "How are you really?"

I told him. I told him all of it. All, except of course that I was in love with him, which was wound and balm at the same time. Even to Mr. Beaufort, who had found me at the bedside of a dead man, I had not told the details of that Christmas night at the hospital. Now it came flooding out, all my fear and uncertainty, the courage which had come to me that night only to be replaced by a benumbing chill which had not left me since.

"I haven't even gone back to the hospital since then," I confessed. "It's cowardly and I know it. I know I should go back, but I can't get up the nerve."

Perry smiled at me across the table, and again the smile was mixed with a greater melancholy, though there was a calm behind it which I could not remember seeing before. He had always kept everyone merry, but I could not recall that sense of tranquility. He reached out and put his hand over mine which lay on the table.

"I know we have never talked about that night in the rain," he said unexpectedly, "but I want you to know that you helped me more than I think you had any idea of. I was miserable and weak then, and you were the strong one. You gave me the courage I lacked to face myself. War has a way of bringing out the best and the worst of people by turns, I think. Let me be the strong one now, and help you."

The calm. The tranquility. So he had faced the fiends which had haunted him and come out stronger. The young man in the wheelchair. An umbrella dropped in the mud. A green bright morning and a small pile of blackberries.

I wanted to say that he had helped me. That he had helped me more than anyone else. That I considered myself in his debt already. But I felt that I could not speak without shedding tears, and I refused to cry. There was no friendly rain shower here to disguise the fact, as there had been that night in the lane. I managed a watery smile, and I squeezed his hand and nodded. It seemed enough.

A death. Bloodstained hands. A rat-catcher's party dress pushed hastily to the back of a closet. And perhaps one day soon another green bright morning?

"Now we will forget about the war for a while," he said, and the world brightened around us. "I can't stay long, but while I do there will be no sadness."

He insisted on treating us all to dinner at the inn that night, and he was warm and kind, and I began to feel the life returning to me in response to the life in him, like a seed under the frozen ground feels the spring approaching and turns towards it. I accompanied him to the train station early the next morning, and before he left he said to me, "Remember, Anna, that you are not alone."

Then he bent his head to kiss my cheek.

Melanie Rose

32

The next evening I went back to the hospital with the others, and it was not the ordeal I had expected and feared, but a return to something which felt right and familiar. The other girls and the nurses welcomed me back and said how glad they were to see me there again, but they asked no questions about why I had been gone, and I had begun to pull myself enough out of my self-pity to know why. They all knew why I had not been there because most of them had been through as great or greater trials than I had. Some had lost brothers, fathers, husbands or sweethearts. How thoughtless had I been in my own sorrow, that I had forgotten theirs?

I remembered years ago, how I had looked out of a hotel window in Florence and thought happily of the linking-together of all humanity. It no longer seemed a happy thing, but we were, if anything, more linked now in our suffering and our endurance of it than ever before. I thought of the little Italian painter who had so idolised his great leader, and wondered what had become of him, if he was still alive. Whatever his fate he was there in my mind, together with a French woman who wept for her sons. My early musings on the connection of humankind had been untried, the wandering thoughts of a girl who had never suffered tragedy beyond the deaths of her parents so early in her childhood that she barely remembered them. They had been tried since then. I thought they had been broken, but instead it seemed that I had been shaken awake from a deep sleep to find them not shattered but realigned into a different pattern. It was not quite the same as I had thought before, not quite so golden, not quite so flawless, yet it held. We were bound. We stood or we fell, together. In the standing there was a great triumph, in the falling a great fear, and for the last several years, we, all of us, had been slipping down the edge of a huge crater.

In April we were informed that women were being allowed to enlist in the Home Guard, and I was not surprised when Violet sent me the news that Gloria had joined up. It was more like her than doing odd jobs for the Red Cross, and, with Hitler choosing to march to disaster in the East for the present, it was not a great deal more dangerous than just living in London.

It was in June that Violet wrote to ask leave to come see me. I said yes of course, only saying that there was no need to ask and she would be welcome at any time. I had missed her a great deal, her quiet manner and honest eyes, and I had worried about her daily since the news of Tristan's death.

She did not come at once, and I began to think she had changed her mind, but then in early July she wrote to say she was coming the following week. I wondered if Gloria would come with her, though she had said nothing. It would be good to see them both. It would be good to see only her.

She came alone, and I hardly recognised her when she stepped out onto the platform at the station. She looked so much older, so much more self-assured. I told myself that it was only natural. I had not seen her since she left Ashford. She had grown up. She stood among the men and women on the platform as their equal, no longer a trepidatious young thing with wide eyes.

I barely know her anymore, I thought. But then she caught sight of me, and the familiar slow, shy smile came over her face, and I saw the old Violet under the skin of this new young woman.

"It was good of you to meet me," she said, coming to give me a hug.

I was still in my rat-catching clothes from the day's work, and apologised for the smell of chemicals and ratty death on my person.

She laughed.

"I've smelled as bad or worse in the last few months," she said. "London smells simply awful these days."

I imagined it did, and had to admit that I preferred my life and the temporary stench of rat-catching from which I could later escape into the fresh air, to hers of stone and cement, death and smoke and unremitting reek. So, I reflected, would she. She had not chosen the path she followed now out of love for life in a city of ashes.

I took her back to the hostel and introduced her to the girls, but it was not long before we left for a ramble over the hills.

It was a perfect summer evening, warm and still, and we wandered in the lanes and fields until long after dark, enjoying the quiet beauty of it all. A nightingale sang in the distance. A dog barked. A shy hedgehog poked its nose out from under a nearby shrub, saw us, and turned into a spiny ball with eyes. We had left the town behind us and were climbing over a stile into a wide green field when Violet stopped at the top and let out a long sigh.

She was looking out over the landscape with an expression that, for reasons I could not understand, made me want to cry, though it was not sad itself. It was a look, I thought, of love and farewell, and I remembered her adoration of Ashford and the country. Life in devastated London must be hard for her. True, we had all lived there for a time, but that was at the beginning, before the smoking piles of rubble became sights as familiar as intact buildings and streets.

"Anna," she said, not looking at me but still out over the country. "Anna, I'm going away." She paused, and I looked up at her from my place on the ground, but said nothing. I found that I was holding my breath, and I made myself let it out, slowly.

"I'm going to France."

Why did I not feel the surprise I felt I should? It was not that I had thought she might do this. I had not considered it. But when she told me, it seemed so like her. I opened my mouth, thinking I would beg her not to go, but all that passed my lips was a question.

"How soon?"

She looked at me then with a half-smile, and with a pang I realised she was giving me the same look she had given the landscape.

"I only waited to see you. I leave in two days. It's an under cover mission I've been training for. I can't talk about it."

I must have looked the question I was thinking, because she shook her head and went on.

"No, I haven't been to Ashford. I couldn't. If I went back I know I would never leave. They don't know about my going. I knew I could trust you to not try to stop me."

I wanted to try to stop her. Wanted to, but couldn't. She trusted me, and the resolute look in her eyes told me it would do no good in any case. I remembered that expression. I had seen it before. Timid she might be, but when that look came over her she did not waver. How had she known that I would not try to stop her? If that were true she knew me better than I did.

I was still standing there staring up at her as she stood at the top of the stile, though I only realised it when she moved to join me on the far side.

"Let's not talk about it any more now," she said. "I want only good memories to think about when I go away."

She wanted images to keep and carry to France with her in the same way I had carried mine of Ashford at Christmas back to my rat-catching. How could I refuse her what I had so clung to? I nodded my agreement and asked no more questions.

We must have walked many miles that night, watched over by a thin sliver of moon which kept disappearing and reappearing between bits of cloud that occasionally showered us with light bursts of warm summer rain. We said no more of France or her going. We said nothing of the war. Sometimes we would speak of Tristan, but always as he was before, of his and Violet's childhood together, of his time at university. We spoke of Perry, of the Beauforts and Mrs. Creeley and Mr. Bertram. We talked of Ashford -- its smell, its warmth, its sense of history and peace.

She left early the next morning. I never saw her again.

Melanie Rose

33

She was one of those declared to be "missing", for they never found her body or any trace of what became of her. In a way it was harder that way, not knowing for sure, and I tried to keep myself from thinking impossible things, like that she had run away to South America under an alias because she couldn't bear to live in England without her brother. I knew it wasn't true or possible. If she were alive she would have gone to Ashford, or let us hear from her. Partly I blamed myself. Why had I not tried to persuade her to stay? But she would have gone in any case. I understood that in my clearer moments, as I also understood that somehow she had known what would happen. Somehow, whether by premonition or simply by a surrendering of herself into the hands of fate, she had known. Her manner when we parted had been that of one who had set aside her fear and looked death squarely in the face, no longer cowed by it. In her way she had been victorious. The war went on. She and Tristan together in their unmarked graves had found their peace before the rest of us.

But I was not ready for the peace of death. I wanted to live. To survive the war and live long and happily. To live at Ashford. I could think of no other home.

The tide began to turn, and we all started breathing again, but hesitantly, like newly released prisoners who mistrust the fresh air as some new trickery of their captors. The hospitals were still full of wounded soldiers, mothers still lost sons and children fathers. The politicians could say what they liked, they could show us lines on maps and talk about pressing forward as much as they wanted. For us, for the little people of the world, the war would not be over until our men and boys stopped coming home with missing limbs, or not coming home at all.

The rats also remained, as wretched, mean, and difficult to catch as ever. Often, as time went on, I felt a great deal of gratitude towards those rats, for they kept both my mind and my hands busy. They kept me sane in a time of insanity.

* * *

I remember exactly where I was and what I was doing the day we heard of the German surrender. Ella and I, who usually worked together on especially difficult jobs, were gassing under the floorboards at a farm where the resident cat had recently died and the rats had decided to have a holiday. We had our handkerchiefs over our faces, and looked, I thought, like the least glamourous types of bandits. Suddenly we heard a noise outside and ran to the window to see what was going on.

It was one of the young boys who worked on the farm, old enough to lift and carry but too young to enlist. He was calling and waving his arms to get our attention. We opened the window, breathing deeply of the clean air, and before we could ask him what was going on he had yelled one word, "Victory!" and run on to tell someone else.

Ella and I looked at each other stupidly, hugged each other, coughed, laughed, and ran outside. It had been more than five years, and now it was over. Soon the soldiers would come home. Life would never be what it had been. Things had changed too much for that. But now perhaps we could begin to start fresh.

We were given the rest of that day and the whole of the next off in honour of the occasion, and last-minute plans were put together for a celebration at the inn.

At the hostel that afternoon I groped to the back of the closet and pulled out my party dress. I had not worn it since that memorable Christmas, when I had witnessed one death and heard news of another. I would smooth out its wrinkles and it would be worn again, and this time there would be no tragedy to mar it, no pain but the pain of memory.

As I dressed I found myself thinking of them all -- of Private Simkins, who had died as I sat beside him, of Tristan, of Violet, of two French boys whose fate I would never know -- as if the dress held memory of them in its folds. For a moment I wavered, hesitant to wear this thing which held so much remembrance of pain to a celebration of victory.

Then I heard the other girls calling me from the next room and I shook off the fancy. The dead were gone and could not be recalled. There was nothing further I could do for them. My concern now must be for the living.

The common room of the inn was brightly lit and crowded. None of the candlelight of that Christmas I had been remembering, but tonight, in spite of my love of candles and the thoughts of Ashford they brought, I was glad of the contrast. It was bright and loud, and there was little opportunity for soliloquy.

It was close to midnight. A young soldier strummed a guitar, and a Captain with a scarred face and the Victoria Cross on his breast stood and began belting out "God Save the King".

Silence came over the crowd as the chatter ceased and all attention was turned to the singer. Slowly everyone began to join in. I heard a man's voice singing to my right above the others which sounded familiar, but it was only when the song was over that I turned and saw that it was Perry.

For a moment I couldn't speak or move, and he stood there smiling at me, enjoying my joy and confusion. Then in an instant I threw myself into his arms, caring nothing for the crowd around us. He picked me up and held me there, my feet inches from the floor, and when I moved my head from his shoulder to look at him he astounded me with a kiss.

At almost the same moment we remembered the milling throng around us. He put me down gently and we let each other go. Suddenly I no longer wanted to be there.

"Perry," I said, laughing a little because it sounded so childish, "I want to go home."

He laughed back at me.

"Come then," he said.

"What? Now?"

"Unless you'd rather stay here."

Through my surprise I shook my head emphatically and followed him to the door.

"There won't be a train for hours," I said.

"It doesn't matter."

We left the inn, and then I saw Mr. Bertram's car. I looked around for someone else. There was nobody.

"But you don't drive."

"I do when it's important. I shouldn't, I suppose. It can be…interesting. Stop staring like that and come with me."

I shook myself.

"I'm coming, but I'm driving.

Ashford

I got into the driver's seat. Perry got in beside me and we drove away. Sometimes Perry slept. Sometimes we talked. Of what hardly matters. Often we said nothing, only kept tryst with the beauty of the night.

We arrived at Ashford in the grey light just before dawn and parked the car at the foot of the garden. Together we sat waiting until, just as the sky was turning pink, we saw the first glimmer of candlelight in the kitchen window. Then we climbed out of the car and started up the footpath. Suddenly I felt nervous. I had not seen them all in so long, and so much had changed. I stopped and looked up at Perry. He must have seen the shrinking in my eyes.

"Adorable coward!"

He took my hand. Together we walked to the front door.

Made in the USA
Lexington, KY
03 November 2011